the
boyfriend
list

also by e. lockhart

fly on the wall

the boy book

(15 guys, 11 shrink appointments, 4 ceramic frogs and me, Ruby Oliver)

the
boyfriend
list

e. lockhart

delacorte press

Published by Delacorte Press
an imprint of Random House Children's Books
a division of Random House, Inc.
New York

www.randomhouse.com/teens

Educators and librarians, for a variety of teaching tools, visit us at
www.randomhouse.com/teachers

The Library of Congress has cataloged the hardcover edition of this work as follows:

Lockhart, E.
The boyfriend list : (15 guys, 11 shrink appointments,
4 ceramic frogs and me, Ruby Oliver) / E. Lockhart.
p. cm.
Summary: A Seattle fifteen-year-old explains some of the reasons for her recent
panic attacks, including breaking up with her boyfriend, losing all her girlfriends,
tensions between her performance-artist mother and her father, and more.
ISBN-13: 978-0-385-73206-2 (trade) – ISBN-13: 978-0-385-90238-0 (GLB)
ISBN-10: 0-385-73206-6 (trade) – ISBN-10: 0-385-90238-7 (GLB)
[1. Interpersonal relations–Fiction. 2. Dating (Social customs)–Fiction.
3. High schools–Fiction. 4. Schools–Fiction. 5. Friendship–Fiction.
6. Seattle (Wash.)–Fiction.] I. Title.
PZ7.L79757Bo 2005
[Fic]–dc22
2004006691

ISBN-13: 978-0-385-73207-9 (trade paperback)
ISBN-10: 0-385-73207-4 (trade paperback)

The text of this book is set in 11-point Baskerville BE.

Book design by Angela Carlino

Printed in the United States of America

September 2006

10 9 8 7 6 5 4 3 2 1

First Edition

For my dear old high school friends,
who were (and still are) excellent and hilarious—
and who never did anything like the bad stuff
people do in this book

Here it is, the Boyfriend List. In chronological order.

1. **Adam** (but he doesn't count.)

2. **Finn** (but people just thought so.)

3. **Hutch** (but I'd rather not think about it.)

4. **Gideon** (but it was just from afar.)

5. **Ben** (but he didn't know.)

6. **Tommy** (but it was impossible.)

7. **Chase** (but it was all in his mind.)

8. **Sky** (but he had someone else.)

9. **Michael** (but I so didn't want to.)

10. **Angelo** (but it was just one date.)

11. **Shiv** (but it was just one kiss.)

12. **Billy** (but he didn't call.)

13. **Jackson** (yes, okay, he was my boyfriend. Don't ask me any more about it.)

14. **Noel** (but it was just a rumor.)

15. **Cabbie** (but I'm undecided.)

Before anyone reading this thinks to call me a slut—or even just imagines I'm incredibly popular—let me point out that this list includes absolutely every single boy I have ever had the slightest little any-kind-of-anything with.

Boys I never kissed are on this list.

Boys I *never even talked to* are on this list.

Doctor Z told me not to leave anyone off. Not even if I think he's unimportant.

In fact, *especially* if I think he's unimportant.

Doctor Z is my shrink, and she says that for purposes of the list, the boyfriends don't have to be official. Official, unofficial—she says it doesn't matter, so long as

I remember the boy and something about what happened.[1]

The list was a homework assignment for my mental health. She told me to write down all the boyfriends, kind-of boyfriends, almost-boyfriends, rumored boyfriends and wished-he-were boyfriends I've ever had. Plus, she recommended I take up knitting.[2]

I still have some doubts about Doctor Z, though by now I've been seeing her for almost four months. I mean, if I knew a fifteen-year-old who sat around knitting sweaters all day, I'd definitely think she had some mental health problems.

I know it's weird to be fifteen and have a shrink. Until I had one of my own, I thought shrinks were just for lunatics, tragics and neurotics. *Lunatics:* insane-asylum can-

---

[1] I think Doctor Z is wrong here. Official does *too* matter, because having an official boyfriend changes everything: how people treat you at school, how you feel when the phone rings, what kind of gum you chew (mint if you have a boyfriend, because you might kiss him at any moment, but bubble gum otherwise). And that leads me to this problem: How are you supposed to know when it's official? Do you have to say "boyfriend" in front of the guy and not have him flinch? Or does *he* have to say it, as in, "This is my girlfriend, Ruby"? Does he have to meet your parents? Or hold your hand in public?

Meghan says, four weeks after the first kiss it's official—but what if you break up for one of those weeks? That happened to my friend Cricket when she was going out with Tommy Parrish.

I was hoping there'd be a set of guidelines handed out in Sex Ed class, but Sex Ed—when I finally got to take it—was all about biology and birth control and nothing about anything that actually goes on between people. Like how to tell what it means when someone forgets to call you when he said he would, or what to do when someone gropes your boob in a movie theater.

I think there should be a class on *that*.

[2] Okay, she didn't say knitting. She said, "something creative," some kind of hobby where I make things. But knitting is the kind of thing she meant.

didates, people tearing their hair out and stabbing horses in the eyeballs and whatever. *Tragics:* people who get help because they've had something really bad happen to them, like getting cancer, or being abused. And *neurotics:* middle-aged men who think about death all the time and can't tell their own mothers to stop poking into their lives.

A lot of my parents' friends are neurotics, actually, but the only other kid I know who sees a shrink (and admits to it) is Meghan Flack.[3] She's had one since she was twelve, but she prefers to call it a "counselor"–like it's not a Freudian psychoanalyst her mom pays $200 an hour, but some fun college girl who's in charge of her bunk at summer camp.

Meghan sees the shrink because her dad died, which makes her a tragic in my book. Her shrink makes her lie on a couch and talk about her dreams. Then he explains that the dreams are all about sex–which later turns out to mean that they're all about her dead father. Ag.

Me, I don't fit into any of my own categories. I'm not a lunatic, or even a neurotic. I started going to Doctor Z because I had panic attacks–these fits where my heart

---

[3] Meghan was never exactly my friend, but she lives two blocks from me and when she got her license in December she started carpooling me to school every morning. Actually, she's not really friends with anyone, except her boyfriend, Bick. He's a senior. Frankly, Meghan's a girl the other girls don't like. When Josh Ballard pulled her pants down in eighth-grade gym class (juvenile, I know, but there you have it), she was wearing pink bikini panties and she turned around like three times in shock, showing them off, before she yanked her shorts back up. And she and Bick went into the bathroom of the bus station when we took a school trip to the Ashland Shakespeare Festival and came out twenty minutes later looking hot and sweaty. Plus she just radiates sex appeal even though she's usually wearing some old flannel shirt, which is very annoying.

would beat really fast and I felt as if I couldn't get enough air. I only had five of them, which Doctor Z says isn't enough to count as a disorder, but all five happened within ten days–in the same ten days I–

- lost my boyfriend (boy #13)
- lost my best friend
- lost all my other friends
- learned gory details about my now–ex-boyfriend's sexual adventures
- did something shockingly advanced with boy #15
- did something suspicious with boy #10
- had an argument with boy #14
- drank my first beer
- got caught by my mom
- lost a lacrosse game
- failed a math test
- hurt Meghan's feelings
- became a leper
- and became a famous slut

Enough to give anyone panic attacks, right?[4]

I was so overwhelmed by the horror of the whole debacle[5] that I had to skip school for a day to read mystery novels, cry and eat spearmint jelly candies.

---

[4] In case you don't know already, panic attacks are episodes where a person feels a sense of massive anxiety; she thinks she can't breathe, her heart rate speeds up, that kind of thing. If a person has them all the time, she probably has a panic *disorder*. Important: Doctor Z says these breathing problems and heart-pounding things can also be symptoms of actual physical problems, so see a doctor, no matter what, if anything like this happens to you.

[5] One of my all-time favorite words. *Debacle:* A sudden, complete, ludicrous downfall.

At first, I wasn't going to tell my parents. I tend to keep them happy, get good grades, come home by curfew and not angst publicly about my problems—because as soon as I tell them one tiny thing about what's going on, they act like it's an earthquake. They can't bear when I'm unhappy. They try and fix it; they'd fix the whole world if they could, just to make me feel better—even when it's none of their business. It's one of the many hazards of being an only child.

So I was keeping quiet about the whole horror that is my life, and we had all sat down to dinner, and my mom was launching into some typical rant about the mayoral election or the rummage sale or some other boring thing she's cranked up about—when suddenly I got dizzy and my heart started banging hard in my chest. I had to put my head between my knees because I felt like I was going to pass out.

"Are you sick?" asked my dad.

"I don't know."

"Are you going to vomit? If you're going to vomit, let me help you to the bathroom."

I hate the way he says "vomit." Why can't he say, "Are you queasy?" or "Is your stomach bothering you?" Anything but vomit, vomit, vomit.

"No, thanks," I answered.

"Then are you depressed?" he wanted to know. "Do you know what the symptoms are?"

"Dad, please."

"Does the universe seem pointless and bleak?" my father asked. "Do you think about suicide?"

"Leave me alone!"

"These are important things to ask. What about this: Do you feel like sleeping a lot? She slept until noon last weekend, Elaine."

"Are you fainting?" my mother interrupted. "I think she's fainting."

"Is fainting a symptom of depression? I can look it up online."

"Have you been eating?" my mother said, as if a light-bulb had gone on in her head. "Are you worried about your weight?"

"I don't know," I said. "No."

"Do you count your calories all the time and think your thighs are fat? Because I saw you drinking a Diet Coke the other day. You never used to drink Diet Coke."

"That was all the pop machine had left." I felt like I couldn't breathe. It was like a rugby player was sitting on my chest, bouncing up and down.[6]

"Eating problems are very common at your age."

"That's not it. My heart is beating really fast." My head was still between my legs, under the table.

"It's okay to tell us," my mother said, sticking her head down under so she could see my face. "We support you. You don't have to be skinny to be beautiful."

"What do you mean, your heart?" asked my dad, sticking his head under, too.

"Fat is a feminist issue," said my mother.

"It can't be her heart," said my father. "She's only fifteen."

"Shut up, you two!" I yelled.

---

[6] Ag! Once you start seeing a shrink, everything you say sounds dirty.

"Don't tell me to shut up," my mother yelled back.

"You're not listening!"

"You're not saying anything!"

She had a point. I told her what was happening.

My mother sat up and banged her hands on the table. "I know. She's got what Greg has. Panic attack."

"Greg never leaves the house," my father said, staying under the table to pick up some bits of food that had fallen under there.

"Greg has a panic disorder. He doesn't go out because he gets a panic thing every time he does."

"I'm not like Greg!" I said, sitting up slowly and trying to take a deep breath. Greg is a friend of my dad's who runs a gardening Web site out of his apartment. He doesn't go *anywhere*. If you want to see him, you have to visit and bring him take-out food. Books are piled up all over the place, and there are like four computers, and nine hundred plants blocking all the windows. He's nice, but definitely insane.

"Greg started out like you, Roo," said my mother. "A little attack here, a little attack there. Have you had more than one?"

"Four others," I admitted, scared but also relieved that what was happening to me had a name.

"I'm making some calls," said my mother, standing up and bringing her plate over to the phone. "You have to see someone about this."

It was no use arguing. That woman is a whirlwind when she gets cranked up. She made Meghan's mother, Sally Flack, who's a doctor and lives down the block from us, come over right away and check my heart and breathing. Doctor Flack was in the middle of dinner. But she came anyway. My mother is a very forceful personality.

Meghan's mom examined me in our bathroom and said I checked out okay[7], and then my mom spent two hours on the phone, describing my symptoms to every single person we know and getting all her neurotic friends to give shrink recommendations.

Doctor Z came recommended by my mother's friend Juana. I think my parents picked her because she was the cheapest: Doctor Z works on a sliding scale—meaning she charges what people can afford to pay. I had my doubts about anybody recommended by Juana, who's a Cuban American playwright with thirteen dogs and four ex-husbands. She seems like a madwoman to me, but my mother says she's an artist. Mom says Juana doesn't worry about what other people think, and that makes her well adjusted.

I say, thirteen is too many dogs for good mental health. Five is pretty much the limit. More than five dogs and you forfeit your right to call yourself entirely sane.

Even if the dogs are small.

My mother drove me to Doctor Z's office on Thursday afternoon. We were early, and she let me drive around the parking lot since I just got my learner's permit, but that turned out to be a bad thing to do right before you go in to

---

[7] Thank god she let me keep my bra on; no way was I showing my boobs to the mother of my carpool driver.

see your very first shrink and when your entire life is crashing down and you can't even talk to your best friend about it because she's half the problem.

Here's why: Your mom will make you insane. You will go so insane the shrink will commit you to a mental hospital the minute she sees you.

We were only going like five miles an hour in a circle around the parking lot, but Mom kept doing these sharp intakes of breath like she was at a horror movie.

"Roo! That guy is pulling out!"

"Uh-huh."

"Do you see him? There, he's backing up."

"Yeah."

"So stop!"

I stopped.

"Don't hit the brake so hard, Roo."

"I didn't."

"You did. I jerked forward in my seat. But it's okay, you're learning. It's practice. Oh!" she squealed, as I started around the parking lot again. "Be careful! There's a squirrel!"

"I wonder where I get my anxiety," I said.

"What, you mean me?" My mother laughed. "It's not from me. Your father is much more anxious than I am. You saw, he thought you were suicidal. Watch the turn there, not so sharp."

Doctor Z's office is in a blank building next to a mall. It's full of orthodontists and dermatologists and all kinds of -ists I never even heard of, but when you get into her actual office, she's hung African art on the walls and covered over the beige wall-to-wall with a deep red rug. Doctor Z herself was wearing a poncho. I kid you not, a big, crocheted, patchworky thing, over a long skirt and Birkenstocks. That's Seattle for you. Psychologists wearing earthy crunchy sandals. She was African American, which surprised me. It shouldn't have, but our family is white as far back on the family tree as I've ever looked, and I guess I picture people white white white unless someone tells me otherwise. Doctor Z wore these red-framed glasses that were too big for her face and gave you the sense that she took her poncho-wearing very seriously.

My mother said, "Hi, I'm Elaine Oliver, we spoke on the phone, blah blah Juana, blah blah blah," and Doctor Z said, "Yes, so nice to meet you, and hello, Ruby, blah blah," and my mother popped off to the mall next door and left me alone with the shrink.

Doctor Z offered me a seat and asked me about the panic attacks.

I told her I was having a bad week.

"What kind of bad week?" she said, popping a piece of Nicorette gum into her mouth.

"Just teenager angst. I'm not shattered or anything."

"Angst about what?"

"I broke up with my boyfriend."

"Oh."

"I don't want to talk about it."

"Okay."

"I just met you."

"Okay. What do you want to talk about?"

"I don't know," I said. "Nothing. I'm fine."

She didn't say anything.

There was a box of tissues on her coffee table that I found annoying. Like she thought I was going to cry any minute. "Aren't you going to ask me about my dreams?" I asked, after a minute. "That's what shrinks do, isn't it?"

Doctor Z laughed. "Sure. I can do that. Are you having any interesting dreams?"

"No."

"All right, then." We sat in silence for a bit. "Tell me something about your family."

This was easy. I have a riff on my family. I spin into it whenever anybody asks me, because my parents are different than most of the people at Tate Prep, the school I've been going to since kindergarten. Tate is for rich kids, mainly. Kids whose parents buy them BMWs when they turn sixteen. The dads are plastic surgeons and lawyers and heads of department store chains and big companies. Or they work for Microsoft. The moms are lawyers too— or they do volunteer work and have great hair. Everyone lives in big houses with views and decks and hot tubs (Seattle people love hot tubs), and they take European vacations.

My folks are madmen by comparison. They send me to Tate on scholarship because "education is everything," according to them. We live in a houseboat, which Kim and Cricket and Nora think is fun but which is actually a horror, because I have *no privacy* (none at all, because the whole house is tiny and built on an open plan, so if I want to be alone I have to go into my microscopic bedroom and shut the door and even then my mom can hear every word

I say on the telephone), and because the area in Seattle where the houseboats are is completely far from anywhere you'd want to go, and the buses run only once an hour. The other problem with the houseboat is bees. My dad runs an obscure garden tip newsletter and seed catalog from his home office: *Container Gardening for the Rare Bloom Lover.* The houseboat has a wraparound deck, and on every square inch of that thing are unusual breeds of peonies, miniature roses, lilies, you name it. If it blooms and you can grow it in a tub of dirt in the Pacific Northwest, we've got it. Which means we've also got bumblebees, all summer long, buzzing around our front door and sneaking in through the window screens whenever they can.

My mother won't set up a bug zapper. She says we've got to live in harmony with them. And truthfully, none of us has ever been stung. Mom is a performance artist (and part-time-at-home copy editor, to pay the bills), which means that she does these long monologues about herself and her life and her opinions about public policy and bug zappers. She gets hysterical onstage, yelling into the microphone and doing sound effects.

She's no longer allowed to talk about me in her shows. Not since "Ruby's First Period" became a major part of a monologue called *Elaine Oliver: Feel the Noise!* I only found out that my personal bodily fluids were her topic on opening night, when Kim and Nora and I were all sitting in the audience together (we were twelve). I died right there, stopped breathing, turned blue and went into rigor mortis in the middle of the Empty Space Theater's second row.

Dad had a talk with her, and she promised never to mention me onstage again.

I've gone through this riff a million times. It's a good way to keep a conversation going, and a good way to prep a friend so she knows she's not finding any BMWs or flat-screen TVs when she comes over. But it sounded different in the psychologist's office. Doctor Z kept going "Umm-hmm" and "Oh, aha," as I was talking, as if she was planning on writing down shrinky-type things as soon as my fifty-minute appointment was up. Stuff like: "Ruby Oliver, obsessed with getting her period, brings it up at first meeting." Or, "Ruby Oliver, fixated on bumblebees."

"Shows considerable anxiety about having less money than her friends."

"Needs father's help to stop her mother from embarrassing her."

"First menstrual period, obviously a traumatic episode."

"Thinking about hot tubs and privacy. Therefore, thinking about sex."

Suddenly, the whole riff seemed weirdly revealing.

I shut up.

Doctor Z and I sat there in silence for twelve minutes. I know, because I watched the clock. I spent the time wondering if someone made that poncho for her, or she made it herself, or she actually bought it at a crafts fair. Then I looked at my low-rise jeans and the frayed edges of the 1950s bowling shirt I was wearing, and wondered if she was thinking mean stuff about my outfit too.

Finally, Doctor Z crossed her legs and said, "Why do you think you're here, Ruby?"

"My parents are paranoid."

"Paranoid, how?"

"They're worried I'll lose my mind and get anorexic or depressed. They figure therapy will head it off."

"Do *you* think you'll get anorexic or depressed?"

"No."

A pause. "Then why do you think you had those panic attacks?"

"Like I told you, it was a bad week."

"And you don't want to talk about it."

"I'm still in the middle of it," I said. "Who knows if Jackson and me are really broken up? Because just the other night he kissed me, or maybe I kissed him, and he keeps looking at me, and he came back to this party I had and was all upset about this thing that happened."

"What?"

"Just a thing. It's too hard to explain. And I don't know why Cricket and Nora have stopped talking to me, but it's suddenly like we're not even friends anymore; and I had a fight with Noel, and I don't know why Cabbie asked me out, or why I'm going. I think he must want something. Oh, and this other guy, Angelo—he's probably never talking to me again—but then again, maybe he will. Basically, I've got no idea what's going on in my own life. That's why I can't talk about it."

I was not going to reach for that annoying box of tissues, no matter what. I took a deep breath so I wouldn't end up crying. "Maybe it's not a bad week," I joked.

"Maybe it's a bad month. But I can't explain it—until I can explain it—and right now, I can't."

"Jackson is your boyfriend?" asked Doctor Z.

"Was," I said. "Until two weeks ago. We might get back together."

"And who is Cabbie?"

"Just some guy. Shep Cabot. We're going out tomorrow night."

"And Angelo?"

"Just some other guy."

"Noel?"

"He's just a friend."

"That's a lot of justs," said Doctor Z. "And a lot of guys."

Before you know it, she had me promising to write up the Boyfriend List. She said it would give us something to talk about next week—and that our time was up.

Adam

1. Adam (but he doesn't count.)

Adam was this boy that I used to stare at in preschool. His hair was too long, that's why. It stuck out behind his ears and trailed down his neck, whereas all the other five-year-old boys had bowl haircuts. I didn't have too much hair myself— it didn't grow fast and my mom was always trimming it with her nail scissors—so I was a little obsessed with hair.

Adam's last name was Cox, and after I had been eyeing him for a couple of months, I named this stuffed bunny I had after him. All the grown-ups laughed when I said the bunny's name was Cox, and I didn't understand why.[1]

---

[1] Another tidbit for Doctor Z's file on my sex mania. "Ruby Oliver: names a stuffed bunny after male reproductive organs. Can't stop thinking about it for even one second, can she?"

Pretty soon, Adam and I were playing together. Our parents took us to the zoo, and we'd spend time after school in the nearby playground, drawing with chalk and walking up the slide. I remember we went swimming a few times at the YMCA, and hung out in a plastic wading pool in his backyard. His cat had kittens, and I got to help name them because I came over the same morning they were born.

And that was it.

We were only five years old.

When I was old enough for kindergarten, I started at Tate Prep and he went somewhere else.

Doctor Z looked down at the Boyfriend List. She didn't seem too impressed with my Adam Cox story. Or maybe it was the list itself she didn't think much of—though it had taken me a lot of work to do. I started the night after our first appointment, in bed in my pajamas, writing on this thick, cream-colored stationery my grandma Suzette got me. It says Ruby Denise Oliver on the top in this great curlicue font—but I never use it, since anyone I'd want to write to has e-mail.

My first draft, I only wrote down Jackson and Cabbie. Then I added Gideon at the beginning, with a question mark next to his name. Then Michael, the guy who was my first kiss—putting him in between Gideon and Jackson.

Then I turned off my light and tried to go to sleep.

No luck.

Well, I wasn't sleeping well lately anyway—but I lay there with this feeling that the list wasn't finished. I remembered that I'd told Doctor Z about Angelo already, so I turned the light back on and squeezed him in between Jackson and Cabbie.

Oh, and I had mentioned Noel to Doctor Z, too—though we were only friends. I stuck him in right after Jackson, just to have somewhere to put him. Then I rewrote the list in nice handwriting and managed to get myself to sleep—but in the middle of the night I woke up and wrote down two more boys and my History & Politics teacher.

Then I crossed them all out.

At breakfast the next morning, I jumped up from my cereal bowl and put one of them back on.

At school, the hallway by the mail cubbies suddenly seemed like an obstacle course of old crushes and rejections. Shiv Neel. Finn Murphy. Hutch (ag). All three in my face before I even got to my first class. I pulled out the list and wrote them down.

All day long, I thought about boys. (Well, even more than usual.) And the more I thought, the more I remembered.

Adam, the mermaid.

Sky, the jerk.

Ben, the golden boy.

Tommy, who surfed.

Chase, who gave me the necklace.

Billy, who squeezed my boob.

Never in a million years would I have expected the list to be anywhere near so long. But by the end of the day, there were fifteen names on there, and the list was all scribbly-looking, with arrows zooming around to show what order the boys should really go in.

It was a mess, so during geometry I recopied it on the stationery in my best writing and threw the old one away.[2] Then I tucked it into a matching envelope to give to Doctor Z.

●

"Why did you stop playing with Adam?" Doctor Z wanted to know.

"I told you, I started a different school."

"Is there something more?" she said, looking at me over those red-rimmed glasses.

"No."

I had liked making the list, it was kind of fun. But ag. What was the point of talking about something from ten years ago that wasn't even important? Zoo trips with Adam Cox and his mom weren't exactly significant to my mental development.

Not that there was anything *else* I wanted to talk about.

I just wanted the panic attacks to stop.

And the hollow, sore feeling in my chest to go away.

And to feel like I could make it through lunch period without choking back tears.

And Jackson. I wanted Jackson back.

And my friends.

"Did you ever see him again?"

"Who?" I had forgotten what we were talking about.

---

[2] A bad idea, you think? Tossing such a document in a public garbage can? Well, all I can say is—you're smarter than me. Which isn't saying much, because I am obviously an idiot.

"Adam," said Doctor Z.

Actually, I did see Adam Cox at an "interschool mixer" two years ago, when I was in eighth grade. Tate Prep is completely small, and so are some of the other private schools in Seattle. The guidance counselors or someone else concerned with our adolescent adjustment decided to try and foster what they called "wider social opportunities for the students, outside the competitive arena of sporting events." Translation: there was going to be a dance. Only they didn't call it a dance, they called it an interschool mixer.

The night I saw Adam Cox again started with us all over at Cricket's house, getting ready and eating cheese puffs. Here's Cricket: cool and blond and wearing pastels, which is a real fake-out because she's the most hyperactive, sarcastic girl I know. Here's Nora: wearing a red shirt that makes her look dramatic; laughing about her boobs—puffing them out and shaking them around, so funny that she had such big ones that early. Here's Kim: sleek, black Japanese hair almost to her waist, a bohemian peasant shirt and no makeup. Here's me, Ruby: just discovered thrift stores, jeans and my zebra-print glasses, plus a beaded blue sweater that cost me $7.89 at a store called Zelda's Closet.

I'm not telling you what I look like in any detail. I hate those endless descriptions of a heroine's physical attributes: "She had piercing blue eyes and a heaving milk-white bosom blah blah," or "She hated her frizzy hair and fat ankles blah blah, blah blah." First of all, it's boring. You should be able to imagine me without all the gory details of my hairstyle or the size of my thighs. And second, it really bothers me how in books it seems like the only two choices are perfection or self-hatred. As if readers will only like a character who's ideal—or completely shattered. Give me a break. People have *got* to be smarter than that.[3]

Anyway, here's us: Kim, Roo, Cricket and Nora. We weren't—and aren't—the really, really popular ones. That's Katarina, Ariel and Heidi, girls my History & Politics teacher[4] would call the ruling class[5] of the Tate universe.[6] And we weren't the bottom of the social strata either—

---

[3] Oh, all right. I know some of you are jonesing for a physical description, and let it not be said that I deprive my readers. I hereby give you Ruby Oliver's five perfect, ideal qualities—and five which I justifiably hate.

    1. No zits/boobs that already flop around more than they should and are destined for sagginess.

    2. Good muscle tone from swim team and lacrosse/tendency to waxy ears.

    3. Long dark eyelashes/bad eyesight and an inability to wear contacts, so glasses always obscure eyelashes anyway, effectively negating them.

    4. Reasonably unhairy body/tummy that will never be entirely flat and might even be said to *stick out* in a completely embarrassing fashion after a large meal.

    5. Cute gap between front teeth/propensity to sweat in nervous-making situations.

    Now you can picture me, right?

[4] Mr. James Wallace. I have such a thing for him. He's from South Africa and has a wild accent and he gets all excited when he talks. He's way too old for me.

[5] He looks great in a bathing suit, too. He's our swim coach.

[6] I know you're thinking I should have put him on the Boyfriend List. Any kind of crush is supposed to be on there. But I left him off on purpose. It's just so stupid to have a crush on your H&P teacher, something that's utterly and completely hopeless like that. Besides, I'm sure if I told her about it, Doctor Z would think I'm a slutty teacher's pet like in that Police song, "Don't Stand So Close to Me." But I'm not. I know Mr. Wallace will never go for me—and even if he did, it would be pretty gross of him. He's like twenty-nine years old. And married.

there's a bunch of kids who lie low at Tate, don't go to parties and dances, don't act in plays or sit around on the quad on sunny days; they seem to just do their work and maybe play some sports or serve on planning committees. Nobody gossips about them.

So the four of us were *reasonably* popular–not *really, really*–but popular enough.

We started hanging around as a foursome at the start of eighth grade, although Kim and I had been friends since kindergarten, when people teased her about what was in her lunchbox (red-bean cake and tofu) and I traded because I don't like peanut butter anyway and that's what my mother always packed. We've been close ever since, and because I was Roo, she became Kanga. Then Nora joined up with us a couple of years later–giggly, bookish, tall and curvy Nora with her huge basement full of dress-up clothes and her ever-present Instamatic camera. Then bawdy, loudmouth Cricket came to school in September of eighth grade, and one day at the start of that year, we were all four sitting in the way-back of the bus on the class field trip to the natural history museum. We were fooling around and laughing and putting our feet up on the seat in front, making fortune-tellers out of folded paper and writing scandalous fortunes inside–until finally a teacher came back and yelled at us, which made us laugh even harder.

Suddenly, after that, Cricket was like our leader. Kim and I were still best friends, sleeping over at each other's houses and talking on the phone for hours every night, but we spent a huge amount of time over at Cricket's house, which is completely deluxe–even bigger than Kim's, and even fancier than Nora's. It has six bedrooms, and a pool, and a sauna, and a hot tub, and two refrigerators. Cricket's room has its own stereo and TV. Her mom works long hours, and Cricket's older sister, Starling, had a car. Starting in eighth grade, we'd ride home with her after school and watch TV and splash around in Cricket's hot tub until our parents came to pick us up before dinner.

At Cricket's house, we did a lot of things you could only do without supervision. Nora baked batches of chocolate chip cookies and we ate them all; we sat topless in the sauna; we copied each other's homework; we watched R-rated movies from her mom's DVD collection; we sent instant messages to boys we thought were hot, using a secret identity.

Actually, we still do most of these things.

At least, we did until the three of them stopped talking to me.

The night I saw Adam Cox again I felt pretty good. We all felt pretty good, but it is a sad truth that I have learned: Dances are generally more fun to think about and get ready for than they actually are when you get there. The "mixer" was a dark gymnasium with some music playing, and a bunch of people I didn't know milling around. That's it. Nora and Cricket went off and danced together, and lots of the girls were dancing in groups—but the boys stood around the edges of the room and splashed each other with punch until a teacher came by and made them stop.

Kim and I amused ourselves by trying to decide which Tate boy we wished would ask us to dance. Shiv Neel.

Billy Krespin. Noel DuBoise. Kyle Greco. "See the guy in the blue shirt?" Kim said. We had been standing there, not dancing, for a long time.

"Yeah."

"He was looking at you just now."

"No, he wasn't."

"No, really."

"That one?" I looked at the boy she was pointing to. He didn't go to our school. He had dark eyebrows and shaggy hair. "Wait! I know him!"

Kim widened her eyes. "Get out."

"I do. From when we were little."

"He's so cute."

Our discussion went on for like ten more minutes, detailing *how* he was cute, who he was cuter than, whose type he was, what we thought of his style, how old he probably was, what movie star he looked like–the kind of thing that's completely interesting when you're talking about it with your best friend, and boring as hell when you read it written down. The end result was that Kim wanted to meet him, and although my palms were sweating and my clothes suddenly seemed all wrong, I walked over to where Adam was goofing around with his friends, Kim trailing behind me.

"Are you Adam Cox?" I asked.

"Maybe," he said. "It depends."

"On what?"

"Why you want to know."

"I'm Ruby Oliver. We used to play together."

"Play together?" One of his friends started laughing

like it was some kind of sex joke. "She says Adam used to play with her! Hey, Adam, did you get some play?"

"Don't you remember?" I asked.

"I don't think so." Adam shrugged.

"What about the mermaid game?" I said. (We used to play this mermaid game.)

"Don't know what you're talking about."

"In the splashy pool," I said, to remind him.

"Beats me."

"You know how your cat had kittens and I helped name them?" I said.

"Yeah, right." He sounded sarcastic. "Meow."

His friends chuckled. "Who's the girl?" one of them called. "Are you two playing kitty cats?"

I took a deep breath. "This is my friend Kim. We go to Tate."

Adam turned his back. "I have no idea what she wants with me," he said to his friends. "Four-eyes."

My face felt hot. "Come on, Kim," I said, grabbing her hand. "Let's go."

Kim has this quality. It's a great quality—until it's turned against you. She's quiet, she doesn't rock the boat. But if you really make her mad, she goes nuts. It's like she spends all this time being a good person, holding up ideals, getting good grades and being nice—and then when someone else fails to live up to her standards, she goes on a rampage. She lit into Adam Cox right there in the middle of the mixer. She walked up and stuck her chin in his chest (he was a lot taller than her), looked up and called him a flabby, low-life, eyebrow-headed mermaid.

"Uh! Get off me!" Adam looked around at his friends as if for help—but they seemed too surprised to do anything.

Kim called him a shallow, phony Barbie doll, and his friends started to laugh.

She was getting started on how he was an uncute, piddle-brained know-nothing, and Adam was looking like he really might hit her, when a tall teacher with a thick brown beard put his hand protectively on Kim's shoulder. "Walk away from it, boys," the teacher said. "Just walk away."

Adam stepped back, but punched the air near Kim's head.

"I said, walk away," the teacher repeated. "You're not going to fight girls in my gymnasium. It's not happening. End of story."

Adam turned to go, but he gave Kim the finger when the teacher looked away for a second.

Kim and I got a lecture about behavior and how if we wanted boys to be gentlemen we should act like ladies, which was idiotic because we didn't want the boys to be gentlemen. We wanted them to think we were pretty and ask us to dance and hold our hands and maybe kiss us in the corner and then send us clever instant messages.

Yes, that's what we wanted, even from boys who were as stupid and mean as Adam Cox and his friends.

I know I should have felt grateful to Kim for defending me, but I was embarrassed. I wished we had been the kind of girls those boys would have been nice to, automatically. I'm not even sure what kind of girls that would have been, why some girls were attractive to boys and others weren't. We were just as cute as Heidi and Katarina—both of whom were dancing with actual ninth graders from Sullivan Boys' Academy. Our clothes were fine. My glasses weren't any worse than Heidi's nose blackheads or Katarina's retainer. But somehow we weren't in that league. It didn't seem like anything that would ever change. Although it did.

The whole Adam debacle did have one redeeming element. Kim and I began our official joint notebook, in which we wrote the most important bits of boy/girl information we knew. We decorated the notebook with silver wrapping paper, and decided that its contents would be for the use of any female we deemed worthy (meaning Cricket and Nora) for purposes of attracting and not immediately repelling the opposite sex—and for understanding what the heck they were all about. We called it *The Boy Book: A Study of Habits and Behaviors, Plus Techniques for Taming Them (A Kanga-Roo Production),* as if it was a nature book about lizards or something.

Which it kind of was.

The very first thing we wrote in it was this: "If you're trying to talk to a boy in front of his friends, don't mention anything too girly. Like mermaids. Or kittens. If you do, he is apt to act like a complete wanker and cause severe injury to your self-esteem. Beware."

Then later, as our understanding of the male psyche increased (well, it's still pretty minimal, but as we got older and read more books and watched more television, at least), we added, bit by bit as our humiliations mounted up: "In addition to mermaids and kittens, the average boy is likely to feel threatened if you mention the following topics: Poetry. Sunsets. Movies with kissing. Notes he's written to you. Notes you wrote to him. Instant messages, likewise. Also e-mail. Past actions suggesting sentiment, such as weeping or saying he likes you. Pet names such as 'snookie' or 'peachie' that the two of you share (if going out). Hairstyles. His mother. Books you liked when you were younger. Dolls. Cooking (if he does it). Singing (if he does it). Failure."

At this point, the first page of *The Boy Book* is so jam-packed with two years' worth of margin scribbles and tiny writing in between the lines that we had to tape an extra page in to make room for all the info on this topic. On the new page, the following addition was made at the start of our sophomore year: "Cramps. Why he didn't call. What he is doing Saturday night. Feelings of any sort whatso-ever." And lower down, in Cricket's rickety scrawl, one of her few additions to this important piece of literature: "When encountered in groups, the human boy, as our se-rious documentation proves, is one of the greatest conver-sational inhibitors known to the female kind. There's nothing to talk to them about! They're jerks when they're with their friends! It's so weird. Scientists are baffled."

I told my parents the story about Adam when I got back from the mixer. I still told them things, then. My dad's first response was to ask me how I thought *Adam* felt.

"Good," I said. "He felt good."

"You don't think he must have felt shy, to be acting like that?" he asked.

"No."

"Sometimes people are mean because they feel insecure about themselves."

"He just didn't like us."

My mother interrupted. "You didn't like *him!*" she cried. "He was a jerk, Roo. Don't think any more about him."

"He's not a jerk," said my father. "He's Roo's friend."

"He's not my friend," I said.

"He used to be," said my dad. "I'm sure he wouldn't act that way without a reason. Poor kid must be having trouble."

"Kevin, the kid is a bully. He used to boss Roo around in nursery school, and he's grown up into a monster. Let her be angry."

"I'm not angry," I said.

"I think it's important to come to a loving place when people are unkind," my dad said. "I want Roo to see that people act badly out of pain."

"I want to call his mother up," stormed my mom. "Kids can't be acting like that. People can't treat Roo like that."

"Don't call his mom!" I cried, grabbing her arm. "Please!"

"Why not? He's a rotten boy and Susan Marrowby-Cox should know about it."

"Elaine, don't label people so much. We don't want Roo carrying around all this fury. We have to teach her forgiveness."

"Hello, Dad. I'm still here," I said.

"If I didn't carry around fury," said my mother, "I wouldn't have a career. People pay to come see me have fury. It's productive. It's cathartic. *Elaine Oliver! Feel the Noise!*"

"Come on," said my father. "You know you have forgiveness issues. Let's not pass them on to Roo."

"Don't bring up my issues. That's not what this is about."

"That's exactly what it's about."

"I think it's about *your* issues," my mother said.

"My what?" yelled my dad—and they were off and running, arguing for the rest of the evening while I sat in my bedroom with my headphones on, trying not to hear them through the paper-thin walls.

I didn't really want to tell Doctor Z about seeing Adam Cox, but she kind of squeezed it out of me by not saying anything, and I finally got bored and told the story. I regretted it afterward.

Because really, the story about Adam at the mixer was a story about Kim. And how we used to be. And how angry she can get. And how angry she is at me, now.

I didn't want to talk about boy #2 on my list either—because talking about Finn Murphy *also* means talking about Kim.

Damn. It's like she's everywhere.

2. Finn (but people just thought so.)

"All right, then," said Doctor Z. "Number two."

I pretended I didn't remember who number two was, and looked over at the paper. "Oh, Finn." I stalled for time. "Why are we doing this?"

Doctor Z shrugged. "It's a way of talking about your history. It's a subject that seems important to you. What can you tell me about Finn?"

"Aren't you supposed to be asking me about my feelings," I shot back, "not quizzing me about my boyfriends?"

"Okay." She uncrossed her legs and leaned forward. "How do you feel?"

"It's not like any of them are even official boyfriends," I went on, "until you get to the end of the list. They're 'almosts.' People I had a crush on, or almost went out with, or they almost liked me, or we kissed once."

"Uh-huh."

"The only real boyfriend I've had is Jackson."

"Jackson."

"Yeah. But I don't want to talk about him."

No way was I telling her about Jackson. He had been my boyfriend for six months—had been my funny, laid-back, mayonnaise-eating, all-the-time-hanging-out, good-kissing, gravelly-voiced Jackson for most of sophomore year. He had fallen asleep with his head on my shoulder. We had driven around the city for hours in his beat-up old car, never running out of things to talk about. He told me he'd never felt this way about anyone before.

He had only been my ex for sixteen days. We'd even kissed since he broke up with me. If I told Doctor Z what happened with that kiss, and with Kim, and the Spring Fling debacle, and the stupid, stupid boyfriend list she made me write that had already made everything even worse—she might not approve when Jackson finally came around and loved me again.

"All right, then," said Doctor Z. "You wanted me to ask how you feel."

"It would be better than talking about a bunch of boys I barely even know," I snapped.

"So how do you *feel*?" Doctor Z looked like she might laugh.

"I feel bored."

Doctor Z didn't say anything.

"Right now. I feel like I'm wasting my time," I said.

Again, she didn't say anything.

I wasn't going to say anything if she wasn't going to. I looked at my fingernails. I pulled at a thread sticking out of my jeans.

"Are you?" Doctor Z finally said.

"Am I what?"

"Are you wasting your time?"

"It's a waste of time to be here, I mean."

"But you're here, Ruby. You don't have a choice. Are *you* wasting the time?"

We were silent. Four more minutes ticked by. I could see the second hand going around the clock.

It was true.

I *was* wasting my time. Because I wasn't telling her anything.

Dad's friend Greg, the one with the panic attacks, stays in his house all day and eats out of delivery cartons.

The attacks were completely scary. I felt sick and weak when they were happening.

Doctor Z looked sweet in her stupid embroidered sweater and red glasses. Not like someone with a PhD in mental illness.

I didn't have anyone else to talk to. None of my friends would even speak to me. Not Cricket. Not Kim. Not Nora. Not even Meghan or Noel.

"Finn is the boy who started this whole horror," I finally said.

In second grade, Finn was not the six-foot blond soccer player he is today. He was a shrimp with white hair who stuck his tongue out the side of his mouth when he was concentrating. I never noticed him much. No one ever noticed him much. Until one day, he was in the school library when I was in there, and he was checking out a book on wildcats that I had read already.

"Did you know that a panther is really a black leopard?" I said.

He looked surprised and clutched the book to his chest.

"And that a mountain lion and a cougar and a puma are all the same thing?" I went on. "It's in there."

"Where?"

"I'll show you."

We bent over the book together, looking at big glossy photographs of lions and ocelots and bobcats in the wilderness. It turned out Finn knew a lot already about the way they train circus lions, and he told a funny story about a cat he knew who could do tricks.

About a half hour later, Katarina and Ariel came into the library and saw us with our heads together over the book. "Ruby and Finn, sitting in a tree! K-I-S-S-I-N-G!" they shouted.

"Shhh," whispered the librarian.

But the damage was done.

For the rest of the year, people teased me and Finn every time we came within two feet of each other.

On the playground: "Ruby's got a boyfriend, Ruby's got a boyfriend!"

In kissing tag: "Ruby, I got Finn for you! Come here and kiss him!"

At lunch: "Finn! There's a chair free next to Ruby. Don't you want to sit with your girlfriend?"

It never died down, because Finn sometimes actually *would* come over and sit in the chair, or he'd give up his swing if he saw me waiting–which only made things worse. He never denied anything either, although I did. When people teased him about me, he'd look over into my eyes in this sweet, shrimpy way that I got to like. After a while, it was as if we had this special secret friendship without ever talking.

After summer vacation, people seemed to have forgotten all about the whole thing. There were new rumors to circulate; the old jokes weren't funny anymore.

But Finn and I remembered. I never spoke to him if I could possibly avoid it. I never chased him in tag, sat near him at lunch, never partnered up on field trips, nothing. I didn't want to risk being teased again, and I'm sure he didn't either–but every now and then I still got that sweet, shrimpy look from him, across the crowded playground.

By the start of sophomore year, he had deshrimped himself. His hair had darkened (though he was still blond), and he had become an athlete. He was quiet, good at computers and science; he played violin in the orchestra. Cute, in a soft, slightly big-nosed way. Not popular, but not geeky, either. Just there. We still didn't talk to each other. It had become old habit by then. If the seat next to him was empty, I automatically didn't sit in it. If I saw him in the halls, I didn't say hi–and he didn't say it, either. No contact at all, besides the looks. Until–

"Know what's true?" Kim said, a week after school

started, tenth grade year. She and Cricket and I were sitting on the grass outside the refectory after lunch, drinking pop and people-watching.[1] Cricket was braiding her long blond hair into tiny braids.

"Tell me what's true," I said.

"Finn Murphy is a stud-muffin."

I opened my Brit Lit notebook and flipped through it. Years and years of pretending Finn didn't exist had made this an automatic reflex. But Cricket nodded. "I think you're right," she said, looking across the quad to where Finn was kicking a soccer ball around with a couple of other boys. "He is a muffin.[2] There's no denying it. But he's a studly muffin. And that makes all the difference."

"I hung out with him after school yesterday," Kim said.

"No way!" Cricket hit her with a straw.

"Way. I went to the B&O to do homework and he was working behind the counter.[3] It was dead in there and his boss was off, so he came out and sat with me." Kim looked down at her lap.

---

[1] The refectory is Tate Prep's pompous way of saying lunchroom. Or rather, *food building*. The school has like eight different buildings, all around a big lawn (the quad). It's pretty posh.

[2] *Muffin*: nice, pleasing, but ordinary. A perfectly fine baked good—but nothing to get too excited about. Not as festive as cake. Not as glamorous as a croissant. Not as scrumptious as a cookie.

[3] The B&O Espresso is a coffee bar. It's like Starbucks, but with fancy cake and old Indian-print cloths on the tables. It's walking distance from the neighborhood full of big beautiful houses where Kim lives. You can sit there as long as you want, doing homework or whatever. We go there a lot when we're not at Cricket's—except that everyone else goes there more than me, because Kim and Cricket and Nora can walk there or ride a bike, but I have to take the bus and transfer twice.

"Was it a *thing*?" I asked.

"Yeah," she said. "I think it was a thing."

"What kind of thing?" Cricket wanted to know.

"A thing thing."

"A thing thing? You mean, really?"

"Maybe."

"Well, was it, or wasn't it?"

"Okay, it was. It was definitely a thing thing."

"Wait a minute," I said. "Are you saying there was kissing?"

Kim looked at the sky. "I'm not saying there wasn't."

"You kissed Finn Murphy?" squealed Cricket.

"Cricket!"

"Kanga had a thing thing/kissing thing with Finn Murphy yesterday afternoon and we're only hearing about it *now*?" Cricket sounded outraged.

"I had a lot of homework," said Kim.

"That's no excuse. You could have e-mailed us, at least," said Cricket. "You are shockingly out of line, young lady. Thing things with stud-muffins that no one else knows about? What is the world coming to?"

"Wait!" I held up my hand. "It is only a real and true thing thing if the kissing thing was *good*."

"Oh, that's right," Cricket said. "Was he a good kisser?"

"Was there tongue?" I asked.

"And was it only a little tongue, or a whole big slurpy tongue?" Cricket asked.

"And where did it happen?" I said. "Did he tongue you right there in the B&O?"

"Or did he walk you home?"

"Or what?"

"I didn't say I kissed him," said Kim, looking pleased with herself. "I only said that he's a stud-muffin this year."

"He's a good kisser, then," said Cricket, standing up to go to her next class. "Look how she's gloating. That's a happy Kanga."

Within a week, Kim and Finn the stud-muffin were going out and it was common knowledge. I had just started seeing Jackson (#13 on the list, my now–ex-boyfriend and the reason for nearly all the debacles of sophomore year). Cricket had a boyfriend named Kaleb from summer drama school, and Nora had—well, Nora can talk about boys with the best of them, and in eighth grade I know for a fact that she tongue-kissed three different guys in a single month—but she hasn't gone out with anyone like a boyfriend/girlfriend thing. I think she'd like to. It just doesn't seem to happen. She takes pictures and rows crew and plays basketball.

Anyway, the sudden glut of actual boyfriends led to many new and fascinating additions to *The Boy Book,* the most important of which was a list of Rules for Dating in a Small School. Here they are:

1. Don't kiss in the refectory or any other small, enclosed space. It annoys everyone. (Hello, Meghan and Bick!)

2. Don't let your boyfriend walk with his hand on your butt, either. It is even more annoying than kissing. (Meghan again.)

3. If your friend has no date for Spring Fling (which is the sort of dance where you need a date, and you get a corsage, and all that) and you already have one, you must do reconnaissance work and find out who might be available to take your friend.[4]

4. Never, ever, kiss someone else's official boyfriend. If status is unclear, ask around and find out. Don't necessarily believe the boy on this question. Double-check your facts.

5. If your friend has already said she likes a boy, don't you go liking him too. She's got dibs.

6. That is—unless you're certain it is truly "meant to be." Because if it's meant to be, it's meant to be, and who are we to stand in the way of true love, just because Tate is so stupidly small?

7. Don't ignore your friends if you've got a boyfriend. This school is too small for us not to notice your absence.

8. Tell your friends every little detail! We promise to keep it just between us.

I was happy for Kim. She had never had an official boyfriend before—and Finn seemed to do all the right things. He called her, he took the bus over to her house to watch movies on TV, he left her notes in her school mail cubby—the place where we usually got notices about

---

[4] Neither Nora nor I got asked to Spring Fling freshman year—Cricket went with Tommy Parrish and Kim went with an older guy named Steve Buchannon—and then later we found out there were perfectly decent boys who didn't go either. We made this rule to safeguard against future such debacles.

assemblies or sports events. He also sat around on the quad with us, and at our lunch table lots of days—which meant that suddenly I was hanging around with this boy that I pretty much didn't speak to.

I could have started speaking to him, of course. That would have been the normal thing to do. I could have tried to make friends with him, like Nora and Cricket did. Not close friends, but goofing-around friends. Cricket called him Blueberry and wouldn't tell him why, and Nora went with Kim to watch soccer games and took action pictures with her Instamatic. But some part of me felt scared of talking much to Finn—or of being seen with him. I could still hear Katarina's singsong voice, "Ruby and Finn, sitting in a tree . . ." and it was hard to break that old habit of avoiding any seat that was open next to him.

Also, I didn't want Kim to think I was trying to steal her boyfriend, if rumors did start up again.

So I was civil. I said hi, and all that, but I basically didn't deal with him if I could avoid it—and he basically didn't deal with me. It was easier that way.

In late October, after Kim and Finn had been going out about six weeks, Kim nailed me on it. "Do you have a problem with Finn?" she asked me. We were eating ice cream bars and sitting on my deck. It was probably the last warmish day before the heavy Seattle rains set in for fall.

"Not at all, he's great," I said.

"Because you hardly even talk to him."

"Really? I hadn't noticed."

"You give him the cold shoulder."

"I don't mean to, Kim. I have a lot on my mind." (I didn't, though. It was an excuse.)

Kim looked concerned. "Like what?"

"Like how Mr. Wallace will never be my husband," I joked. "I'm pining away for him, but he's such a Marxist, he'll never marry me."

"Roo."

"All I want is to be Mrs. Wallace and have little South African–accent babies—"

"Roo!"

". . . and look at him in his Speedo swim trunks every morning before I go off to work, while he stays home with the kids. But he'll never go for it."

"He's already married."

"Oh, yes. That's another problem. My love is unrequited. Must you add to my misery?"

41

"Roo, seriously—"

"Mr. Wallace doesn't love me. I need some more ice cream."

"—what is the deal with you and Finn?"

Now, the intelligent girl would not have told. The intelligent girl would have said, "Nothing, I swear on my life," and started talking to Finn like a normal person.

But me, no.

I decided to spill my guts about this minor weirdness from second grade that clearly no one remembered except me and him. I told Kim the whole story. How we had fun looking at the wildlife book, how Katarina and Ariel teased us, how he'd save swings for me and had still given me that sweet, shrimpy look as recently as last semester.

Kim was my best friend. I wanted her to understand why I had been so weird with Finn. I figured I could tell her everything.

But now, I wish I hadn't.

3. Hutch (but I'd rather not think about it.)

Doctor Z didn't say anything while I told the story about Finn. She just nodded, and looked at me.

At home, my dad is always asking me questions about stuff, wanting to know the details of all my friends and their lives. And my mom is always interrupting anything I'm talking about to tell me stories about when she was young, and how she felt just like I do—only worse. It was weird to talk and have someone listen quietly for half an hour. When I was finished, Doctor Z looked up at the clock and said it was almost time to go, anyway. "Come back Thursday," she added, "and we'll do number three."

Number three on the list is Hutch.

I almost didn't put him on at all. I'd rather forget the

whole thing. Not that anything drastically bad happened. It's just that Hutch has become a leper at Tate,[1] and though I'm sure I'd be a better person if I was comfortable talking to all kinds of people, and if I treated everyone equally—I'm not, and I don't. It's sad that he's a leper. He eats alone. He sits in the back corner of the classrooms. I'm sure he suffers unspeakable indignities in the locker rooms. And I do feel bad when people sneer at him. But he also creeps me out, like he's gone into this zone of his own Hutch weirdness and he's thinking his private heavy-metal thoughts and absolutely choosing not to wash his scraggly heavy-metal hair[2] or brush his grayed-out heavy-metal teeth. He says bizarre things if you ever talk to him— as if he's making in-jokes about stuff that only he could possibly understand.

Like this: Nora sat next to him in Brit Lit. She came in one day wearing a black hoodie. She's going through an all-black phase. Hutch went, "Nora Van Deusen. Back in black! I hit the sack."

"What?"

---

[1] *Leper:* Leprosy is a supercontagious disease that rots your body so badly that bits of you *actually fall off.* In the Tate Prep universe, a leper is someone with no friends.

[2] I know there are people who don't have access to clean water and toothpaste and that my life is super privileged. Mr. Wallace talks a lot about poverty and the way it's a cycle of problems that stop people from being able to get or keep high-paying jobs; they can't clean up and dress up to get the job that they *could* do if they only had it—that kind of thing.

But this was not the case with John Hutchinson aka Hutch. He lives in a huge house in a gated community; I know, because it's right near Jackson's house, and I'd see him go by sometimes, his mom driving a Mercedes.

He was *choosing* to have dirty hair.

"Back in black! I hit the sack."

"What are you talking about?"

"Never mind." Hutch shook his head like Nora was the town idiot.

"Did you say, hit the sack?"

"Yeah."

"As in, get in bed, hit the sack?"

"That's not what I meant," Hutch muttered. "You wouldn't understand."

"It better not be what you meant," said Nora.

"Whatever," he said. "I'm just joking with you."

"It's not a joke if nobody gets it," Nora snapped, opening her notebook.[3]

Stuff like that. He'd say things that sounded creepy, but you couldn't figure out what he meant, so if you got mad, you seemed like an idiot. He'd appear to be quoting something, or referring to something—but he'd also know that you'd have no idea what it was—so why was he even talking if he was intentionally not communicating? He was basically talking to himself.[4]

In fourth grade, Hutch was a laughing, popular boy. I didn't know what happened, exactly, that made him change. I couldn't remember when he switched from cool

[3] For your edification, I related the Nora/Hutch conversation to my dad, and he explained it: Hutch was quoting a line from a 1980 song by a metal group called AC/DC. The scene of my dad singing this song (he knew all the lyrics) and playing air guitar is just too horrible to describe, so I'll leave it to your imagination.

[4] That was so Hutch. His heavy-metal quote is not even heavy metal that other metal people are listening to, so there's literally no one in his entire generation who could possibly have a clue. He's into *retro* metal.

guy to leper, but in fourth he was cool and he put a huge bag of gummy bears in my mail cubby with a note. I remember feeling happy that someone so confident and golden would notice me. The note didn't say much. Actually, all it said was "From J.H. (John Hutchinson)," and for a second I worried that he put them in the wrong cubby and they were really meant for Ariel Oliveri–who had, has and probably always will have the mail cubby next to mine. When I looked up, though, Hutch was grinning at me across the hall, so I knew they were for me. I felt weird, because we hadn't spoken to each other very much, but I spilled some bears into my pocket and ate them very slowly over the course of the day, thinking to myself, Hutch likes me, I got a present from a boy, Hutch likes me, he gave me candy. I said it over and over and over in my mind.

The rest of the bears I took home and hid under my pillow. They lasted a week. I'd eat them at night and think about how I sort of had a boyfriend, and how my dad would kill me if he knew I was eating candy after brushing my teeth.

But although Hutch and I did sit by each other one day at a school assembly, and although I sent him a valentine with two extra candy hearts taped onto it on Valentine's Day, and although we smiled at each other a bunch for several weeks in a row, we were basically too young to do anything more.

Then one day, I noticed Ariel taking a big bag of gummy bears out of her mail cubby.

"Are those mine?" I asked her.

"No. See?" She showed me a card attached to the bag. It had her name on it. Hutch was smiling from the other side of the hall.

"So he was breaking up with you?" asked Doctor Z. It was two days later, our third appointment.

"I guess."

"It was hard to tell?"

"I think he was *replacing* me."

"Oh. Were you angry?"

"No. Why do you say angry?"

"I thought you might be, from the way you described Hutch being a leper with gray heavy-metal teeth."

"I was just playing around with my vocabulary. I'm not angry."

"I don't mean to put words in your mouth."

"I think I felt relieved. Like it was nice that he liked me, but I didn't know how I was supposed to act, or talk to him, so it made me nervous whenever I was at school. When he started liking Ariel, then I didn't have to angst about it anymore."

"Talking to a boy who liked you made you anxious?"

"Doesn't it make everyone anxious?" I asked. "Isn't that a universal sentiment? You know, sweaty palms, shallow breathing, the symptoms of love?"

"Maybe. But we're talking about you. A person who has panic attacks."

●

None of my friends had spoken to me since Spring Fling. I didn't even know why.

Not exactly. Not really.

I mean, it was obviously about the whole Jackson debacle, but why Cricket and Nora were on Kim's side, I had no idea.

On the Tuesday after my first shrink appointment, someone finally *had* spoken to me, and that was worse than the silent treatment. I was in line for a pop and a sandwich that I could take out back to the bench by the library when Nora came up behind me.

I think she would have left if she had seen it was me, but her tray was on the counter and she had grabbed a bottle of juice before she realized I was standing there—so she was kind of stuck.

"Are you mad about something?" I asked her, when the silence was more than I could bear.

She looked at me and sighed. "Isn't it obvious?"

"About that Xerox?"[5] I asked.

"No. Give me some credit already."

"Then enlighten me."

Nora's voice dripped with venom. "You can't make out with someone else's boyfriend, Roo," she said. "That's so against the rules."

"What?"

"Rules for dating in a small school? You wrote them yourself."

"We didn't make out," I said. "It was only a kiss." (This, about the Jackson debacle. It's a long story. For now, just know that there was ex-boyfriend kissing involved,

---

[5] More on that later. Right now, I just want to say again: *Never* throw anything away in a school garbage can that you want to keep secret. Never.

and that Jackson was now attached to Kim, making him technically off-limits.)

"Same thing." Nora shrugged. "He belongs to someone else."

"It was Jackson," I said. "What was I supposed to do?"

"That doesn't matter."

"He's my boyfriend more than he is Kim's."

"Not true."

"We went out for six months."

"Well, you're not going out anymore."

"He kissed me back."

"You started it, Roo. People saw you."

"But there are circumstances!" I cried. "Can't you think how I must have felt?"

"I never thought you could betray one of us like that. It's so wrong." Nora flashed her lunch card and stepped out of the line, walking fast like she wanted to end the conversation.

I followed. "Don't you even want to hear my side of it?"

"What side could you possibly have?" She flipped her hair over her shoulder and turned away.

"So you're dumping me as a friend? Without even talking about it?"

"I don't even know what kind of friend you are, anymore," she said, turning back.

I couldn't believe she was saying this. After what Kim had done to *me*.

"Neither does Cricket," Nora added.

"What?"

"You always talk about official and unofficial," Nora went on. "And then you just forget about it when it stands in the way of something you want. It's like you never even think about how there's other people, and they have feelings."

"What about Kim?" I was almost yelling. "What about *my* feelings?"

"Kim didn't cross any lines. She kept to the rules, completely."

"Says her."

"She did."

"How do you know?"

"She'd never do anything like what you did. Everyone saw you kissing him. It was humiliating for her, didn't you think of that?"

"For her?" My throat was closing up and my vision was blurring. I felt like I was going to have another panic attack. "I have to go," I said, and bolted out of the refectory into the fresh air, where I followed Doctor Z's instructions and took deep, calming breaths and tried to think relaxing thoughts, even though I felt like I was going to die, right there, leaning against the rough brick of the building.

●

That afternoon's appointment with Doctor Z helped a bit, actually. I told her the Hutch story, and a little about how nobody would talk to me, and it suddenly hit me: I had become Hutch. Well, that makes it sound too dramatic (and also insane). But in the course of two weeks I had gone from reasonably popular to a bona fide leper–

and when I talked, I might as well have been talking to myself, since nobody seemed to understand a thing I said.

The next day at school, I was determined to face the refectory again. I hadn't eaten lunch there in more than a week, but even lepers need their calories and somehow learn to stand it, eating by themselves in dark corners with their books propped up in front of them, while everyone else is joking and laughing. I couldn't keep eating on the bench behind the library forever.

At the salad bar, I took a long time making the same combo I always have for lunch. Lettuce, raisins, fried Chinese noodles, baby corn, cheese, black olives, ranch dressing. I fiddled around adding things here and there until I saw Cricket, Kim, Jackson and Nora all sitting down at our regular table.

Finn, who used to sit with us, was eating with a bunch of guys from the soccer team.

Hutch sat in a corner wearing an iPod and looking very interested in his hamburger.

There was a table full of boys right in front of me: Shiv (#11 on my list), Cabbie (#15), Matt (Jackson's best friend), Kyle (another of Jackson's friends), Pete (Cricket's new boyfriend) and Josh (who was just obnoxious). I couldn't bring myself to face them.

Katarina and her set would probably tolerate me—I mean, I didn't think they'd push me off my chair or anything—but I knew that they'd all heard Kim's side of things, and heard her call me a slut in Mr. Wallace's class, and that I wouldn't exactly be welcome at their table. Plus Heidi was there, and she's Jackson's old girlfriend, and the last thing I wanted to face was the weird new sisterly sympathy she had started affecting (like the same man hath done us both wrong and we should share our sob stories), when less than two weeks ago she'd been completely jealous and catty because I was the girlfriend of the boy she liked.

Beyond the sophomore/junior tables, over by the window, seniors.

I scanned the room for people I knew from the lacrosse team, but couldn't see anyone.[6]

I could feel Kim ignoring me through the back of her head. Jackson nudged her with his shoulder and she laughed. The inside of my chest felt cold and hollow.

I stood stupidly with my tray of raisin salad, staring at the two of them like I was looking at a train wreck in slow motion. I couldn't move my eyes away. I felt like everyone at school could see my heart breaking, blood pouring out of my chest and sloshing down across my shoes and gushing under the tables.

And nobody cared, because they thought I deserved it.

●

Two weeks ago, back when I had a life and friends and a boyfriend, I had ended up eating lunch with Meghan

---

[6] Re: the lacrosse girls. The ones in my grade form kind of a sporty clique that I've never been part of. Maybe because I swim in the fall, and most of them play soccer. Or because I'm goalie, so I'm not out on the field with them. Or because (now) I'm a famous leper/slut. Anyway, they're nice, but they're *serious;* they're on leadership committees and honor rolls. Not a lot of opposite-sex action is going on. They just don't make me laugh, and I don't make *them* laugh either.

They're very team-spirity.

against my will. She blindsided me at the salad bar, look-ing unbearably cute in what must have been Bick's crew T-shirt and a pair of old corduroys.[7] "Ruby Oliver, are you deaf? I've been calling your name from our table for ages!"

Sticking out her lower lip in that pouty way she has that makes all the other girls love to hate her,[8] Meghan had pointed to a table filled with seniors.[9] Prime refectory real estate, right by the windows. Meghan is the only sophomore who eats there every day. Actually, she's the

---

[7] *Bick:* His real name is Travis Schumacher. But have you ever seen the movie *Taxi Driver* with Robert De Niro? Scariest thing ever. De Niro plays a kind of sad, likable psychopath named Travis Bickle. If you ever hear people going, "You talkin' to ME?" they're imitating *Taxi Driver.* Anyway, Travis Schumacher . . . Travis Bickle . . . Bickle . . . Bick. There you go.

[8] Some more complaints against Meghan:

1. She's always rubbing the back of her neck and moistening her lips with her tongue like she's in a porn video (not that I've ever seen one). Whatever. It's practically indecent, and very annoying, and boys seem to like it. At least, they stare at her when she does it, even if she's only asking them about a homework assignment.

2. When people are sitting around in a hot tub (a very Seattle thing to do at parties), she's always in a bikini. The rest of us wear T-shirts and boxers.

3. When we were reading *Othello* for Brit Lit, our teacher was trying to point out to us that it's basically impossible to know anything for sure and certain, and asked if there was anything anyone in class felt we absolutely knew for sure. Meghan was the only one who raised her hand and this is what she said: "I know my boyfriend loves me."

[9] I don't think the senior girls like her much either. They eat lunch with her, but you never see her leaving with any of them, or sitting with any of them on the quad unless Bick is there too. After all, Meghan is a sophomore making time with the punk-rock-loving, rugby-playing, crew-rowing spiky-haired seniorness of Bick—and in a school as small as Tate, that seriously reduces the number of old-enough, hot-enough potential boyfriends for the senior girls.

only sophomore who *ever* eats there, partly because she has no friends in her own year, but mainly because she's been Bick's girlfriend since last summer.

"Oh," I said. "I didn't hear."

"Come sit with us," she said, grabbing my arm and pulling me to her table. I looked around for Jackson, Cricket, Kim and Nora and waved an "I can't help it, she's a madwoman" wave at them from across the room.

"Bick, this is my friend Ruby that I carpool," Meghan said, sitting on Bick's lap so I could have her seat. "You know, the one I always talk about."

I smiled and nodded–but inside, I cringed.

"Hey," Bick said. He flashed his smile at me, then leaned back into a discussion of some party Billy Alexander was having next week. Meghan whispered in my ear from her spot on his lap, pointing the seniors out like they were trophies she was proud of winning. "Debra, Billy, April, Molly, the Whipper, Steve."

Of course, I already knew who all of them were.

For a second, I felt bad for Meghan. These people weren't her friends. Not really. Except for Bick, I could see that they basically pretended she wasn't there.

I wasn't her friend either. Most of the time, I was annoyed that Meghan even existed. And here she was, dragging me over to meet her boyfriend, like the two of us were so close. Was I really "the one" she always talked about?

Carpool was different. I gave Meghan gas money every month, and she agreed to show up on time. It was a business relationship. We'd sing along to the radio and make up stupid lyrics, mostly. Sometimes we'd try on each other's lip gloss or copy each other's math homework. I'd bring these oatmeal cookies my dad used to make (before my mom went macrobiotic) and we'd eat them for breakfast.

I only knew about her shrink and her dead dad because she was very up-front about it and probably told everybody she knew. She'd bring it up at 8 a.m., while we were swinging through the Starbucks drive-thru window on our way to school—the same way she'd talk about her singing lessons or where Bick took her on Saturday night. She had never been over to my house or anything.[10]

I choked down my salad as fast as I could. Meghan and Bick started tickling each other. A few of the senior girls rolled their eyes and stood up to leave. I took their cue and got up myself.

I hooked up with Kim and Nora on the quad, where I

---

[10] Except for one time, when her Jeep broke down just as she was dropping me off. She came in and called the tow truck. After that, she went into our bathroom, did whatever in there, came out and asked me, "Where's your bathtub?"

She seemed almost freaked out when I told her we didn't have one. Just the shower. I mean, it's a *houseboat*. There's not a lot of room—hello? Kim, Nora, Jackson and Cricket have been in my bathroom a million times and none of them ever said anything about it, and Meghan's comment definitely gave me one of those moments that I have every now and again at Tate, where I think: *I am not the same as these rich people.*

But after the weirdness of that one interaction died down, it was actually okay having Meghan over. We watched some goofy stuff on after-school TV until her mom picked her up.

gave them a blow-by-blow of the whole weird lunch. We speculated about whether Meghan was still a virgin.

Two weeks later, not even Meghan was talking to me.

I took my raisin salad over to the table where Hutch sat listening to his headphones. We didn't speak. I read my H&P homework while I ate.

4. Gideon (but it was just from afar.)

Gideon Van Deusen is Nora's older brother. He graduated already and took a year off, driving around the country visiting unusual places like the world's only corn palace and the museum of surgical science. Then he's going to Evergreen, deferred admission.

I liked him starting in sixth grade, when he was in ninth. He had intense eyes. It began when I was over at Nora's house playing video games. Gideon must not have had anything better to do, because he was hanging around with us. He told a funny story about how the week before, his youth group leader from church brought in two loaves of banana bread for everyone to eat. One loaf was nice—fluffy and sweet; the other was all sunk in and weighed like a pound. The leader said the second one had been made with the exact same ingredients as the first–only they were put together in the *wrong order*. He told the kids that the wrong order made the whole banana bread taste gross, and it was the same thing with sex. If you had sex before marriage, you had done it in the *wrong order*. And *you* would turn out gross. But if you did everything in the *right order,* meaning not having sex until your wedding night, you came out wonderful, fluffy and sweet. Angel material. So all the boys and girls should save themselves for marriage.

I thought this story was exotic because (1) my family doesn't go to church, and before Gideon told this story I hadn't even realized that Nora's family did, and (2) when Nora went into the kitchen to get us all some pop, Gideon told me that he liked the gross, heavy banana bread better.

"Why?" I asked.

"Because you have to think for yourself," he said. "You can't believe everything people tell you."

"But did it really taste better?" I wanted to know.

"Not really," he said. "Politically."

"Okay, but did it at least taste kind of good? Or were you faking?"

"That's not the point, Roo. You know that." He said it like he had confidence in my understanding.

"Oh yeah," I said. "I know."

It was then that I decided that Gideon was fascinating, and wrote "Ruby loves GVD" on the bottom of my sneaker that same night. I started tracing over it with a purple Magic Marker, whenever I was bored in class.

Within a week, it had become this nice lettering that looked like calligraphy.

Then one day, I put my feet up on the chair in front of me during assembly.[1] Nora saw the sole of my shoe. "You mean GVD, Gideon, my brother?" she cried.

I blushed.

"Ag! I can't believe you like my brother!"

"She *loves* him," squealed Kim, grabbing my foot and turning it so she could see. "That's what she wrote."

"Don't angst, I swear I won't tell," promised Nora.

"I won't tell either," added Kim.[2]

"But since when do you like him?"

"No, since when does she *love* him?"

"He's a nice guy." I yanked my foot away.

"Nice doesn't make you love someone," said Kim.

"Ugh," said Nora. "He's gross."

"He's different," I said. "He wants to be a musician."[3]

---

[1] I am an idiot, I know.

[2] Doctor Z says, maybe I *wanted* it to be discovered and put my feet up subconsciously on purpose. I say, if I did that, I must have been some kind of eleven-year-old masochist (someone who enjoys pain) because I had never been so embarrassed in my life; it was so embarrassing it actually hurt. And if I was a masochist at eleven, then imagine how messed up I am by now. Just commit me to the asylum and be done with it.

Doctor Z says, Maybe there were larger reasons you wanted people to know. Maybe it was a way of being honest about your feelings?

I say, Maybe not. Maybe I'm just an idiot.

And she sighs and says, Okay, Ruby, I can see you don't want to talk about this right now. We can come back to it when you're ready.

[3] Okay. Now I know that every single ninth-grade boy in America wants to be a musician. They play air guitar in their bedrooms and pretend they're rock stars. But I didn't know that, then.

"You think he's cute?" asked Nora, wrinkling her nose in disbelief.

Of course I did. He was—and is—incredibly cute in a messy, rebellious way. "Not really," I said.

"His eyebrows grow together."

I loved his eyebrows. I still love his eyebrows. "It's more his personality," I said, feeling stupid.

"And he never cleans his room. There's mold growing around up there."

He was unusual, I wanted to say. He had better things to do than be tidy. "Don't tell!" I begged.

Nora shook her head like I had revealed an interest in bug collecting, rather than her brother. "I said I wouldn't."

But of course she did. Or at least, she hinted. That very afternoon, as I was heading across the quad to the library, Gideon caught up to me. "Roo, I hear there's something on your shoe that I should see," he said.

"What?"

"On your shoe."

"There isn't anything."

"I think there is."

"No, there isn't."

"Come on, let me see it."

"No!"

"Please?"

"It's nothing, leave me alone."

He tackled me, laughing, and I fell onto the grass, squealing, completely embarrassed, oh, the horror, having never told a boy I liked him, ever in my life, smelling his Coca-Cola smell, laughing and almost crying and worrying that he would notice I didn't have any boobs yet and that my sneaker was stinky.

As soon as he saw what was written on the bottom of my shoe, though, Gideon's face changed. I don't think he knew what it would say, just that it would be something about him. And here is the reason that I still like Gideon Van Deusen, with his lovely hairy eyebrows: He didn't laugh, or tease me, or tell me to get away. He sat up very seriously, and said, "Roo, that's so sweet. I'm flattered."

"It's only a doodle," I said, looking down at the grass.

"No, it's nice. I'd much rather it was you writing about me on your shoe than that annoying Katarina."

"Really?" Katarina was considered adorable by almost everyone.

"Sure," he said. "Write on your shoe all you want. Write a whole book. Fine by me: I'd be famous!"

He slung his backpack over one shoulder, and was gone.

I didn't speak to Nora for a week.[4] Then she said she was sorry, and I got over it.

Nothing else ever happened between Gideon and me. I'd see him at the Van Deusens' house. My heart would thump.

He'd say, "Hi, Roo," and be too busy to ever say much else.

---

[4] If I had half a brain, this episode would have cured me of putting any of my thoughts about boys into writing. It is way too dangerous. But I obviously didn't learn my lesson then, and haven't learned it now. I keep doing it, even after what happened with the Boyfriend List. Look at what you're reading now! Pure evidence of my idiocy.

But I still think about Gideon. I wonder if he was lonesome driving across the country on his own. I think of him playing guitar out on a wide prairie by a campfire, or learning to surf off the coast of Big Sur. I asked Doctor Z if it was psychologically questionable to like a boy three years older who will never, ever like you back.[5] Or to still think about a boy who has never even touched you, except for that tackle on the grass.

"It's normal to have fantasies, if that's what you're asking," said Doctor Z.

"It doesn't *feel* normal," I said. "I thought about him even with Jackson."

"When you and Jackson were out together?"

"No. When I was alone."

"What did you think?"

"Just what it would be like, if he liked me."

"What would it be like?"

"Like everything was easy," I said, after a minute. "Like everything was simple."

"Life isn't simple, Ruby."

"But it would be," I said, "if I . . ." I found I didn't know what to say.

"Did it feel simple with Jackson? When you first liked each other?"

"For about a month," I said. "Then it got complicated."

"A month isn't very long."

"I know," I said. "But it was a good month."

---

[5] Mr. Wallace is *fourteen* years older than me. At least. But I don't need to ask Doctor Z to know that liking him is certifiably insane.

Jackson Clarke put a tiny dead frog in my mail cubby near the end of eighth grade. I knew it was him because Cricket saw him walking away with a small, dripping Ziploc bag. We couldn't figure out if the frog was meant to be mean (and if so, why would he single me out?)—or if he had a crush on me, and this was his idea of a gift (maybe he was a science dork?).

He was a grade ahead of us, so I had never thought much about him until then. We didn't have classes together. His face was square and freckled, his hair dark brown and inclined to curl if he didn't keep it short. His eyes crinkled up when he laughed. He was tall and had a raspy voice. And he was obviously an asshole. My cubby smelled like frog for three days. I wondered if he had done it on a dare.

I felt sad for the frog and buried it under a bush outside the main building. In fact, the whole episode kind of shattered me, and I couldn't figure out why. I looked at Jackson in the hallways, trying to gauge whether he hated me, or liked me, or was even thinking about me. But he never looked my way.

Summer came, and fall again—but Jackson wasn't in school. We heard his dad had business in Tokyo, and had moved the whole family there for a year. Jackson would go to school in Japan. I didn't think about it much—until he came back, first day of sophomore year.

I love the start of the school year. I think about what clothes to wear. I use a nice black pen in my fresh, new narrow-ruled notebooks. I crack the spines on my books.

Everyone looks different, and everyone's the same. Jackson was like four inches taller than he had been (which was already pretty tall), and he was wearing jeans and a T-shirt that said something in Japanese. I saw him laughing with a bunch of other juniors in the hallway as I walked in the door, and suddenly–I knew I liked him. The sun came through the window and lit up his hair. He had a bandage around his wrist like he had sprained it. His backpack was at his feet, looking new and stiff.

I think I had liked him all year, while he was away.

In movies, there are always misunderstandings before the hero and heroine get together. He seems like he hates her, she thinks she hates him, he maybe courts her a little, they connect for a moment, then she misunderstands something and hates him again for most of the movie, despite various appealing things he does to try to win her. Or it's the other way around, he seems like he hates her because he misunderstands something *she* did.

And then it turns out they were wrong. They love each other madly. And that's the end.[6]

Well, I know I watch too many movies. I should be working with my dad in the garden or helping the needy or getting a little fresh air. But I fully expected that if romance ever did come my way, it would only be after a long stretch of hints and confusions and tiny gestures and

[6] Movies where the couples hate each other half the time: *Ten Things I Hate About You. One Fine Day. When Harry Met Sally. You've Got Mail. Intolerable Cruelty. The African Queen. Addicted to Love. Bringing Up Baby. The Goodbye Girl. How to Lose a Guy in 10 Days. As Good As It Gets. French Kiss. Groundhog Day. A Life Less Ordinary.*

retreats; or even after a stretch of full-out dislike, which would suddenly morph into true love when all parties least expected it. Don't get me wrong. I wasn't expecting violins and sunsets and roses, at least not in any great numbers. I just figured on a little drama.

But no. When it came to me and Jackson, everything was easy right from the beginning. So easy, it almost didn't seem like romance.

It was the middle that was difficult.

And the end was even worse.

Another thing that happens in the movies: They all have these dramatic crises where everything looks bleak and you think the couple will never, ever get back together. But then they realize they can't live without each other, and in the end they live happily ever after.[7]

It's all a lie. When you hate someone you used to love, and you think he's done something awful–he probably has.

You're not going to love him again.

He's not going to apologize, or come back to you.

He probably doesn't even ever think about you at all, because he's too busy thinking about someone else.

Face it. There's not going to be a happy ending . . . at least not with this hero. So don't go mooning around

---

[7] Movies where after breaking up, it turns out the man actually loves the woman madly and can't exist without her: *Pretty Woman. An Officer and a Gentleman. Bridget Jones's Diary. The Truth About Cats and Dogs. Reality Bites. Jerry Maguire. Persuasion. High Fidelity. Say Anything.* Plus, *Notting Hill, Grease, Four Weddings and a Funeral* and *Runaway Bride*—only the woman comes back to the man.

thinking that your breakup is only the crisis before the big romantic scene, because I'm here to tell you that it's not. When you are dumped, you are dumped, and the guy isn't going to change his mind and realize that suddenly he loves you instead of that girl he's flirting with in the refectory, now that he's free.[8]

Jackson smiled at me that morning, first day of school.

The day after that, he said, "Hi."

"Hi back," I said.

The day after that, he said, "Hey, Ruby, what's up?" and I said, "Not much."

But the day after that, and this was before Kim had even noticed Finn and his stud-muffinly qualities, I got a note in my mail cubby. I used to get notes all the time, from Kim and Nora and Cricket, but this one was folded up into quarters, with a funny drawing of a frog on it. I knew who it was from, somehow, without even opening it.

Inside, it read: "The frog was for Awful Ariel Oliveri (AAO). Not for you. Sorry." And then: "P.S. I just got my license. Need a ride home?–Jackson."

My dad came to pick me up after school. He waited in front of the main building for forty-five minutes. I was long gone.

We went to Dick's, this drive-in burger place that I'd always heard juniors and seniors talking about, but that I had never been to, since at that point none of my friends

---

[8] Doctor Z says it's a good anxiety release to express your anger. So in the interest of preventing further panic attacks, I'm venting. Not too bad, huh?

was old enough to have a driver's license. I'm a vegetarian, so I got fries and a milk shake. Jackson got a burger and a root beer float. We sat on the hood of his big old boat of a car, a Dodge Dart Swinger that had once belonged to his uncle.

He told me a little about Japan. He spoke some Japanese for me when I questioned his ability.

I did my riff on my family.

He said he wanted to row crew this spring, but he was worried, since he hadn't been in a boat since before he went away. He talked about the food in Japan, and said he ate raw fish. I said that French fries were better with Dijon mustard.

He said he was a ketchup man all the way.

I said, If you tried the mustard, you'd become a convert.

He said, I have tried mustard.

I said, Was it Dijon?

He said, No. Just regular.

I said, Then you haven't tried it.

Oh, he said, have you tried mayonnaise?

I said, Mayonnaise is gross.

He leaned in close, and said, Really, you don't like it?

Ick, I said.

And he kissed me, and whispered, "I love mayonnaise."

He kissed me again—

—and I didn't feel like a loser

—and I didn't worry that I couldn't kiss right

—and my glasses didn't get in the way

—and I didn't wonder if he'd tell his friends

—and I didn't wonder if it was a joke.

This is Jackson Clarke, I thought, who put the frog in my cubby. This is Jackson Clarke, who used to have braces. This is Jackson Clarke, who's been to Japan. This is Jackson Clarke, whose tongue tastes like root beer. This is Jackson Clarke, who used to seem ordinary. This is Jackson Clarke.

I kissed him back.

He drove me home.

And there actually was a sunset.

5. Ben (but he didn't know.)

Ben Moi was at my summer camp after sixth grade. He
didn't know I existed.

"There's nothing to say about him," I told Doctor Z. "I
liked him. Everyone did. He was golden."

"What did you like?"

I didn't have an answer. "There was something about
him. He always had a girlfriend. He had like three different ones over the course of the summer."

"But not you?"

"One time, I sat next to him at a camp sing-along and
I pressed my leg against his, trying to be sexy, but he kept
moving it away. He was going out with this girl Sharone,
anyway."

"Then why did you put him on the list?" Doctor Z was chewing Nicorette again. I can't imagine her smoking, but she must light up like a fiend as soon as her workday is done; she chews that gum like an addict.

"I used to think about him all the time," I told her.

"Like what?"

"Huh?"

"What did you think?"

"I don't know. Normal stuff about a boy you like."

Doctor Z was quiet for a minute. "Give me a hint, here, Ruby," she said. "Something."

"I just wanted to go out with him. Like when I got dressed in the morning, I'd think about whether he'd like me better in jeans or shorts; or I'd wonder if he'd notice I put mustard on my French fries, and would he realize that I was unusual?"

"Did you think about kissing him?"

"Not really."[1]

"Did you like talking to him?"

"We never had a conversation. Except once, he told me my shoe was untied."

"Did he make you laugh?"

"No."

"Was he talented, or interesting?"

"Um. Not particularly, I don't think."

"Did he make you feel special?"

---

[1] I honestly didn't. Because I never even kissed *anyone* until I was thirteen and three quarters. This is an embarrassing and sadly true fact, made even worse by the fact that the guy I kissed was totally gross and I didn't kiss anyone else after that until the end of my freshman year.

"He made me nervous. I always felt sweaty and ugly whenever he was around."

"Really?" Doctor Z leaned forward. "Why like someone who made you feel sweaty and ugly?"

"He was hot," I explained. "Ben Moi was just the guy that you want as your boyfriend."

"But why?"

"Can't you just want someone?" I asked. "Does there have to be a reason?"

"This is therapy, Ruby." Doctor Z sounded exasperated. "It might be helpful for you to try to articulate something about something."

So I told her the truth: I thought about how it would be to have such a perfect, popular boy for a boyfriend. How with someone like Ben Moi, I'd know I was all right. I'd know I was pretty. I'd know my clothes were right. I'd know someone wanted me.

"Validation," she said.

"I guess so." It didn't sound so good when she put it like that—but it didn't sound untrue, either.

"And when you had a boyfriend, with Jackson, did you feel all those things?"

"Yeah," I answered. "I did."

It was amazing how simple it was, how fast Jackson and I went from strangers to spending every minute together. He met my parents. I met his parents. We did homework together. We kissed for hours. His dog liked me.

I never imagined that having a boyfriend would mean having someone to hang around with, someone who'd drive over to my house to eat dinner with my parents on a Wednesday night, stay to play Scrabble, then sit on the couch reading his history assignment while I did my math. In fact, what it was like with Jackson was completely different from how I thought about dating in the first place.

I always figured a boyfriend would ask me out, then pick me up on Saturday night. Me and this imaginary boyfriend would do boyfriend/girlfriend things that you don't normally do with other people: walk on the beach, go for a scenic drive, see a foreign movie, go dancing. We'd have plans. I never thought he'd swing by on Saturday morning to see if I wanted to run his errands with him and we'd end up buying fifteen lollipops at the drugstore and opening them all and having blind taste tests.

I always thought I'd get dressed up to go out with my boyfriend. I'd put on lip gloss and eye shadow and fishnet stockings. But Jackson would be waiting for me when I left swim practice in sweats and a T-shirt, and I'd jump into his car and we'd immediately start making out, and he'd touch my chest through the wet swimsuit I had on underneath and I didn't care that I had no makeup on, or that my boobs were squashed together by the suit, or that I smelled like chlorine, or that I had worn the same T-shirt the day before. I was just happy to see him.

He left me notes in my mail cubby nearly every day. "Here's a penny," he wrote. "Maybe it'll bring good luck. Or you could buy a kiss from me. Or stick it on your nose, throw it in the air and catch it, buy a penny candy, give it to a man who is down on his luck, give it for a tip to a bad waiter, get it cold and drop it down your shirt, swallow it

and get a free ride to the hospital, cover the face of someone's watch so they're late to class, give it to a cowboy and
have him shoot a hole in it from fifty yards away, put it in
your shoe for a trick on yourself. And I have only just be-
gun to brainstorm! Your big bad penny-totin' man, Jackson." Or, "I left at 2 PM today because we got out of chem
early. Why? There was a fire and a hurricane and light-
ning in the chem lab. Oh, sorry, did I alarm you? Really,
it's 'cause Dimworthy said, 'Clarke, you're so damn smart.
I've taught you everything I know already about the mysteries of the universe. Get the hell outta here and go shoot
some pool.' So I left. See you tomorrow. Jackson."

I loved those notes. I still have all of them. Back when
I dreamed of having Ben Moi as my boyfriend, knowing I
was pretty, knowing I was wanted—those things were true
when I was with Jackson, and I didn't worry.

Now—after everything that's happened—I am tempted
to say it was too good to be true. But it *was* true, for at least
a month. And when I think of what I want from a
boyfriend, or a lover, or a husband someday—what Jackson and I had, at first, that is the thing that I want.

The other way that Jackson was like Ben Moi was that
he had had a lot of girlfriends. Before he went to Japan, he
had gone with Beth, Ann and Courtney—all girls in his
year—and once I started going out with him I developed
Beth-Ann-Courtney radar. I could sense whenever one
of them was in the room, what she was wearing, how
pretty she looked. It seemed so weird that those Beth-Ann-
Courtney lips had touched Jackson's lips; that they'd held

his big, freckled hands; that he thought they were beautiful; that he thought they were interesting. Before Jackson was my boyfriend, those girls had seemed perfectly nice. Now, they seemed shallow and overly flirtatious. They irritated me, laughing and being charming and having nice legs and no glasses. I wished they would all three disappear.

Jackson and I had been going out for six weeks when an incident happened that inspired a whole new section of *The Boy Book* entitled "Traumatic Phone Calls, E-mails and Instant Messages: Documented Painful Episodes Involving Communication Technology."[2]

Here's what happened: I was over at the Clarkes' house on a weekday around six p.m. We were doing homework and playing video games in his room. The phone rang as Jackson was on his way downstairs to get something, so he asked me to pick it up.

"Clarke residence," I said.

"Um, is Jackson there?" It was a girl's voice.

---

[2] Three sample entries from *The Boy Book* under this heading:

1. Kim e-mailed Finn re: that fight they had about her missing his soccer match, and he never e-mailed her back the whole weekend. Kim checked her e-mail every ten minutes and didn't pick up her phone because she didn't want to talk to him unless he'd read what she wrote. Then on Monday, Finn said he never got her e-mail, it must have gotten lost. But later he said he never checked his e-mail. Which one was it? The guy didn't even get his stories straight.

2. Cricket's drama-school boyfriend Kaleb, who lasted only six weeks (good riddance!) was always creating a sense of mystery around his answering machine. He would never check his messages if she was there to hear them— like there was going to be some big secret phone call from another girl on there. Cricket said she was pretty sure there were only messages from his

"He's downstairs," I said, wondering who it was. "Do you want to hold on?"

"Um, yeah," she said.

I handed the phone to Jackson when he returned. He sat down with his back to me. "Hey, what's up?" he said into the receiver.

There was a pause.

"I can't talk now, someone's over."

Why wouldn't he say *Ruby's* over? I wondered. Ruby, my girlfriend, is over. That's what he should have said.

"Please don't say that," Jackson was almost whispering. "No, no, it wasn't that way."

What way?

"It's not anything you did, I told you," he went on. "Listen, it's not a good time. Can I call you later? . . . Yes, I still have your number."

Then he hung up, picked up the Xbox joystick and went back to killing aliens.

I looked down at my math homework, but I couldn't concentrate. Who had been on the phone?

---

friend Mike, or some similar Neanderthal, and that Kaleb was only faking her out by pointedly ignoring the message machine, and it must have meant a lot to him to do so—because by nature he was a compulsive message checker. He checked his cell like every hour.

3. In the period between Kaleb and Pete, Cricket got a ride home from a basketball game with Billy Alexander, and she was all excited because they were sitting in his car talking, parked in the driveway in front of her house. It seemed like he was going to kiss her, or ask her out, or something. But then his cell phone rang, and he answered it, and said "Dude!" a lot, and waved at Cricket as if to say "See you later!" So she got out and went inside—and that was that.

What were they talking about?

Why didn't he tell me?

It was none of my business, really. He could get phone calls from whatever girls he wanted.

Or maybe it *was* my business; after all, I was his girl-friend, and wasn't I entitled to know if there were other girls he had intimate conversations with, conversations that were obviously about important feelings?

"Who was on the phone?" I asked, trying to sound bored.

"Oh? Just now? Heidi Sussman," he said. Heidi from Katarina's set.

"What did she want?"

"She's upset about something or other. I told her I'd talk to her later."

"Upset about what?" I hoped I sounded concerned for Heidi and not overly nosey.

"Oh, she's always upset about something. Who knows what it is, this time around," Jackson said, killing aliens all the while.

What did that mean, always upset about something? What was going on with Jackson and Heidi Sussman? Was he just interested in the video game, or was he deliberately leaving out information?

I tried to be interested in the dying aliens.

I tried to be interested in my math.

I tried to think of another thing to talk about, a movie or something.

"Why is she calling *you*?" I finally asked.

"We used to go out," he said. "You knew that." Still killing aliens.

"No," I said. "I didn't." I couldn't believe I'd been sitting next to Heidi in class for weeks, doing a scene with her in Drama Elective, saying hello in the halls, all without knowing that she had been Jackson's girlfriend.

Jackson turned to look at me. I'm absolutely certain he knew I didn't know, and actually meant me not to know for as long as he could hide it from me. "It was in the summer. We were hanging out at tennis camp," he said. "We broke up before school started."

"How long before?" I asked.

"I don't know. A couple of days," he said. "The day before, I think."

"The same week we started going out?"

"Yeah, I guess. She keeps wanting to talk about it."

"What does she say?"

"I don't know." Jackson chuckled and put his arm around me. "I wish she'd leave me alone. I've got better things to do." He nuzzled my neck. "I'm not gonna call her back, if that's what you're worried about."

I couldn't blame Heidi for wanting to talk. I mean, Jackson had barely caught his breath before replacing her with a new girlfriend. Suddenly I felt dirty, like I'd been involved in something ugly and mean without my knowledge. "You should talk to her," I said. "It's only fair."

"You think so?"

"Yeah. There shouldn't be any bad feelings."

"All right," he said. "I'll call her later."

I did mean what I said. If I was Heidi, I'd want the boy to talk to me. It would drive me insane if he kept saying he'd call and never did. It would be so unfair. But at the same time, when Jackson told me he was going to the B&O for coffee with Heidi after school on Friday and wouldn't be picking me up at swim practice, I was completely shattered. He was going out with his ex-girlfriend! The girl he had been kissing and thinking was pretty and special and wonderful only six weeks ago. I felt jittery all through practice, and swam badly. My dad picked me up, and I asked him to take me to a five o'clock movie so I wouldn't have to think about Jackson and Heidi—so I wouldn't give in to the temptation to call his cell phone while their big coffee discussion was still going on. But typical Dad, if we were having an afternoon together, he wanted to bond. "Why don't we go to that B&O place you like?" he suggested. "I've always been curious about it."

"I'm not hungry," I said.

"Really? Aren't you usually starved after practice?"

"I am, but all they have at the B&O is cake," I said. "It's like a coffeehouse."

"You can have cake," my dad said. "I won't tell Mom. Besides, if they brew a serious cappuccino, I want to know about this place."

He turned the wheel and got off the freeway at the exit for the B&O. I didn't know what to say. I didn't feel like I could explain the situation to him, but if we showed up while Jackson was having coffee with Heidi, it would look like I was spying on them. And even though I actually *did* want to spy on them, I knew I wasn't supposed to want to—and was supposed to be trusting of Jackson and unjealous of Heidi—because that was the cool way to be. Plus this whole thing of them talking was my idea in the first place, so supposedly it would be insane for me to be jealous.

My dad found a parking space and we marched into the B&O, him all beaming and talking about the teen hangouts of his youth, the merits of different coffee beans and the importance of whole milk in cappuccinos. I scanned the room, my heart thumping.

But Jackson wasn't there.

And neither was Heidi.

Some artist types sat at a table for six, sucking down espresso. Kim was at the counter, writing an essay on her laptop. Finn was behind the register, wearing a black apron and gazing at her with big moony eyes.

Where were Jackson and Heidi? Had they seen Kim and decided to go elsewhere for more privacy?

Or had they finished up quickly and gone their separate ways?

Or had they finished up quickly because they had fallen madly back in love with each other and were even now making out in the Dodge Dart Swinger, steaming up the windows?[3]

My dad clapped Kim on the back in greeting and

---

[3] Don't I sound paranoid? When I told this story to Doctor Z, I tried to make a bit of a joke out of me thinking these insane things about Heidi and Jackson making out. I said something like "Oh, I know this is insane stalker paranoia, but these crazy thoughts went through my head."

But Doctor Z said, "They don't sound crazy to me, Ruby. It sounds like your trust had been shaken by Jackson's hiding the fact that he'd gone out with Heidi." And while the way she put it was pretty touchy-feely, and I found it kind of annoying to have her repeating my feelings back to me, I did appreciate that she didn't try to talk me out of it, or tell me it probably wasn't true.

started quizzing Finn about professional-level milk-steaming methods.

"Where's Jackson?" I whispered to Kim. "How long were they here?" She knew the whole situation, of course.

"He *never came*," Kim whispered back. "Finn has been here since three o'clock."

"What?" I could handle it when I knew where they'd be—but now it seemed like Jackson and Heidi had gone off to do some private thing between the two of them, like I didn't even exist. I wondered if he'd even lied to me about what the plans were.[4]

My dad was having the time of his life, so pleased to be in his own daughter's hangout, drinking cappuccino with her real live friends. He ordered cake. He flipped through the ads for rock shows in the local free paper and imagined he was going to buy tickets to something. I tried to be a good sport and act like I was enjoying myself. He's a sweet dad, he completely is, and he meant well and was trying to bond, and who can blame him for not noticing that I was nearly out of my mind with anxiety?[5]

---

[4] Either these thoughts are insane and paranoid (see previous footnote) and I am a superpossessive jealous lady, *or* they are completely justified reactions to a tense situation in which there is a completely reasonable possibility of betrayal.

And either Jackson was entitled to a private life and it was none of my business, or (as his girlfriend) I was entitled to an explanation of what he was up to when it concerns other girls. Which is right? I have been in therapy for several months now and have no answer.

[5] Know what Doctor Z said when I told her this about my dad? "You *can* blame him, Ruby. Blame away, if you're angry."

"I wasn't angry."

Jackson called when my dad and I got home. He wanted to come over. We sat on the deck, even though it was cold, to get some privacy.

He and Heidi had played tennis, for old times' sake. They were so evenly matched and it was something they used to do together. Then they had talked in the restaurant area of their country club. Heidi wanted to get back together with him, Jackson said. She didn't understand why things had broken off so suddenly. But he didn't want to. Heidi was fun and superbeautiful and all, but she wasn't that interesting. "I told her I was with you," he said, taking my hand. "Roo, please don't feel upset. I've never felt like this with anyone before I met you."

"Me neither," I said.

"It sounds like he wasn't noticing the signals you were sending out. Did you hope he'd be more responsive?"

"Maybe he did notice completely and was just trying to give me space and not intrude on my business," I said. "So there."

Doctor Z chewed her Nicorette. "But either way, you wanted him to bring it up, isn't that what you're saying?"

"No. It's not like I want to talk to my *dad* about that kind of thing."

"You don't want to?"

I tried to actually think about it. "No. . . . I mean, yes. . . . I mean, I did want to. I guess."

"Is there a way you could have helped that to happen?"

Oh, she makes me so annoyed sometimes. "Yes ma'am," I said, sarcastically. "I could have told him how I felt. That's the *right* answer, isn't it? That's what you want me to say."

She was quiet.

"Therapists are all the same," I went on. "Tell people how you feel. It's like the solution to every problem. Blah blah blah."

"Have you *had* another therapist, Ruby?" she asked me.

We sat there for the rest of the session.

"Good," he said, leaning in. "I hoped not."

We kissed in the cold air for a long time.

But the truth is, I never felt the same after that. Not really. Look back and reread what Jackson actually said when he told me about his afternoon with Heidi. True, he said he wanted me, had never felt like this before. But he also said Heidi was superbeautiful and fun, and that they'd played tennis for old times' sake, because they were so well matched, blah blah blah.

Now, if your entire focus was on making your *new* girlfriend feel better about your feelings for your *old* girlfriend, would you mix your declaration of love in with nostalgia about tennis games and the superbeauty of the old girlfriend?

No.

You would only do that if you were still thinking about the beauty and the tennis.

It's not that I think anything happened with Heidi that day, or that Jackson was lying about how he felt toward me. It's more that I realized he had this history with other girls, and I couldn't stop him thinking about them, and he *would* think about them even when he was looking me in the eye.

It shattered something inside me that hadn't been broken before.

So then I had Heidi radar on top of the Beth-Ann-Courtney radar.

And now I have Kim radar.

All the way until the end of the school year, I could

barely walk across the quad without evil vibrations attack-ing me from all directions. Ag! Kim on the staircase! Heidi in French class! Triple threat of Beth-Ann-Courtney in the library, wearing pastels and having good hair days! The evil was everywhere—and just writing that sentence proves to me that I'm seriously messed up and thank goodness my mother made me start seeing Doctor Z because I am obviously about to go off the deep end, even after all this time has passed.

Believe me, I know the actual truth is that these are all nice girls. Some of them even used to be my friends. And I firmly believe that women should not get all cruel and petty with each other over men, because how on earth will we run companies and countries if we're preoccupied with someone else's big boobs in a pink sweater set?

In H&P, Mr. Wallace was talking about this kind of problem (we were covering the feminist movement), and I so agreed with the points he made about what he called "self-defeating antagonism between members of oppressed groups." Translated from Wallace jargon, that means that if people want to fight for their rights and actually see some action, then they have to stick together and not be pissy with each other about little things.

My problem is I can think whatever I think—girl power, solidarity, Gloria Steinem rah rah rah[6]—but I still feel the way I feel.

Which is jealous. And pissy about little things.

---

[6] Gloria Steinem. A famous feminist. My favorite thing she said: "A woman with-out a man is like a fish without a bicycle."

Maybe the stuff that went wrong between Jackson and me *made* me feel insecure, and that's why I got jealous of Beth/Ann/Courtney/Heidi. Or maybe I felt that way to start with out of some sour meanness in my soul, and my neurotic jealousy is part of why things went wrong in the first place. I'm not sure.

I only know that I felt this way—and I still feel this way. Even though Jackson and I are broken up.

I wish I felt different. I'd like to walk into the refectory and not have any radar at all. I'd like to just go in there, make my raisin salad and eat my damn lunch without a care in the world. But I doubt if it's happening anytime soon. Right now I'm still lucky to get through a meal without a panic attack.

6. Tommy (but it was impossible.)

When I was in seventh grade, Tommy Hazard was a blond California boy, a top surfer for his age. He wore bright color-block shorts and had a smile that showed his slightly crooked front teeth. His voice was low, so when he talked it was like you were the only person in the world who could hear it. He had a blue ten-speed bike and would ride me on the handlebars. He smelled faintly of chlorine from his family's swimming pool, and the two of us would spend warm afternoons with our feet in the water, holding hands and watching the clouds go by.

In eighth grade, Tommy Hazard had a Mohawk and rode a skateboard. He could play electric guitar, and hung out at an underage punk-rock club downtown. He always had a novel in his back pocket, and he bought his clothes at vintage shops, like I did. He seemed tough, but on the inside he was vulnerable and kind.

By the time I was in ninth grade, Tommy Hazard was old enough to drive, and he rode an old Vespa scooter. His helmet was painted with zebra stripes, and I'd ride along behind him with my arms around his narrow waist. Tommy's hair was shaggy and dark, and he wore an old sharkskin suit and a narrow tie; he had a darkroom in the garage of his family's house, and when he was alone he'd go in there and develop the most beautiful black-and-white photographs. He took a lot of pictures of me, saying he didn't want to miss a moment.

Then I met Jackson, and now there is no Tommy Hazard. He's just gone.

Kim still has him, I bet. Her Tommy was always the same, whereas mine was always changing.

We invented Tommy Hazard on our seventh-grade day hike, which was basically a bunch of harassed teachers trying to move our twelve-year-old butts up a mountain and get us to like it, while we all gossiped and wished we were at the mall.

We ran out of stuff to talk about halfway up the trail.

We walked in silence for a mile or so; then we made up Tommy Hazard. He was the perfect boy. The boy who was never obnoxious in math; the boy who never threw spitballs, or pushed anyone on the playground; the boy with clear skin and a sense of purpose; the boy who never did anything stupid in gym class or the talent show; the boy who knew the answers in class but didn't say them;

the boy who was beautiful; the boy who was cool; the boy who could have any girl he wanted—and all he wanted was me. Or Kim.

Tommy became our boyfriend from seventh grade on, and we'd hold him up as an ideal whenever we talked about actual boys. For example, Kim went out with Kyle for two weeks in eighth grade, and when she broke up with him, she said, "He was okay. But let's face it, he was no Tommy Hazard." Or I'd catch sight of a cute boy in a movie theater, and say, "Kim! Look over there! I think it's Tommy Hazard!"

During the long periods where no boys liked us and there weren't even any decent boys for us to like, we made plans with Tommy. Tommy took me to see old movies at the Variety. He took Kim out in a canoe. He put his arm around me in the theater. He stopped paddling and kissed Kim, out there in the middle of the lake.

These were the Hazard core elements, agreed upon by both of us:

He never embarrassed us.

He did something more interesting than watching TV after school.

He was a great kisser.

He held our hands in public.

And he was utterly confident, but weak in the knees whenever he saw us.

Beyond that, we personalized him. My Tommy was always changing: surfer boy, skate punk, mod—those were only the top three. Sometimes he was a boisterous athlete; sometimes a quiet poet. He was the boy everyone knew;

or the boy no one besides me ever noticed. Sometimes he had a tasty foreign accent; sometimes he played piano. He was muscled. Or he was slight. He was white, black, Asian, anything.

Kim's Tommy Hazard was always the same. She refined him over the years, adding and subtracting minor qualities, but fundamentally he was consistent. Tommy Hazard à la Kim had traveled all over with his family; he was an adventurous eater (she loves spicy food and gets irritated by people who only eat pasta and peanut butter); he was a boatsman (she sails); a film buff; a good student. He was older, he was popular, he was tall.

"He's out there, somewhere," Kim said to me, the summer after ninth grade. We were walking through the open-air market, down by Puget Sound, looking at woven bags and bead earrings and handmade wooden puzzles. We had been talking Tommy Hazard for the past half hour. "I really do think so," Kim went on.

"What do you mean, out there?"

"I don't mean Tommy Hazard, like he looks the way I think he looks," she said. "I mean someone who's the one for me, and I'm the one for him."

"True love."

"Yeah, I guess." She fingered a batik pillow, shopping while she talked. "But more like destiny. Or fate. I know it's silly, but I kind of feel that if I keep thinking about him, someday he'll show up."

"How will you know? Love at first sight?"

"Maybe. Or it could sneak up on us. My mom says one day she 'just knew' that my dad was the one."

"Really? How?"

"A feeling," said Kim. "They had been dating for nine months. But they got married three days later. Once she knew, she knew." I couldn't picture the Doctors Yamamoto doing anything so romantic.[1]

"I don't know if there's a *one* for me," I said. "I think I might like variety."

●

In tenth grade, poor Finn the stud-muffin still had to compete with Tommy Hazard. Kim liked Finn, she did, but he was a bland-food eater (not even pepper) and had never traveled out of the Pacific Northwest. He wasn't "the one." He was "for now."

In any case, after I told her the whole story about me and Finn in second grade, the sweet shrimpy looks and the "sittin' in a tree" and all that, I did make an effort to talk to him like a normal person. On top of the weirdness of having avoided him all those years, though, it was strange trying to have a conversation when I knew stuff about him like whether he had chest hair (no, but a little on the stomach), what he smelled like (soap) and what his room looked like (he still had a stuffed panda on his bed). My first few attempts were failures.

"What's up, Finn?"

---

[1] Mae Yamamoto is a brain surgeon. She talks superfast, and she's always doing six things at once. You go into Kim's house and her mom is chopping vegetables, washing the cat in the sink, consulting on the results of someone's biopsy over the phone, cleaning out the fridge, changing out of her work clothes and yelling at Kim for overusing the credit card, all at the same time. You have to see it to believe it.

"Not much. How are you?"

"Good."

"Good."

Like that.

Tate Prep has all these charity initiatives—you have to do a certain amount of community service each term. In late October, all the sophomores grouped together to create a Halloween party for kids at a local YMCA on a Saturday afternoon. We had to come in costume. I was a cat in a black minidress, fishnet stockings, a fake-fur jacket and ears. Cricket was a cricket, which involved antennae and a green leotard. Nora was Medusa. Kim was a ballet dancer in a pink tutu.

Most of the boys were firefighters or cowboys or something else manly-manly, but Finn was a black cat too—at least that's what he looked like. He wore a black turtleneck and black jeans, a long tail and gloves that had claws on them. His face was all black greasepaint, and he had a hood with ears coming out of it that looked like it was probably leftover from a Batman costume the year before. It was a very un–Tommy Hazard kind of outfit.

Mr. Wallace was organizing us. He had retained his dignity and dressed as Albert Einstein. This involved wearing a suit (he's usually in khakis), graying out his hair and wearing a sign on his back that said "$E=mc^2$," in case no one could tell (which no one could, until we read the sign). "You kitty cats," he said, pointing at me and Finn, shortly after we arrived at the YMCA, "you man the face-painting table."

Finn and I sat down at a table filled with odds and

ends of makeup heisted from the drama department storage room. "He called me a kitty cat. Can't you tell I'm a panther?" Finn said to me. "Look at my claws." He held his hands up.

"You'll have to take them off to put makeup on the kids," I said.

"Damn. Then I'll look like a kitty."

"What's wrong with a kitty? I'm a kitty."

"No insult to kitties," said Finn, smiling. "That's just not what I am. I'm a panther."

"I have to tell you," I said. "You look pretty kittyish to me."

"Hey, did you know a panther is really a black leopard?" he asked. "If you look closely, you can actually see the spots underneath the black."

"You got that from me," I said. "From the nature book."

"Nuh-uh. I got it from watching the Discovery Channel."

"Finn! I told you that in second grade. Don't you remember, in the library?"

He changed the subject. "How can I be more panthery?" he mused, sorting through the makeup on the table. "Do you think I need whiskers?"

"Your face is black. You can't put whiskers on." Kim and Nora were across the way from us, setting up a pumpkin-carving table.

"Red. What about red whiskers? Then I'd be scary." He took off his gloves and picked up a lipstick. "Where's the mirror?"

I handed it over. He opened the lipstick and started drawing fat red lines across his face. He had no idea how to do it. It was a disaster. "You look like Freddy Krueger,"[2] I said. "Especially if you put the gloves back on."

"Damn! Now I'm some Freddy Krueger kitty cat." He was laughing. "Maybe I should give up and be a dude in black."

"Let me help." I took a tissue and some cold cream and wiped the makeup off Finn's cheeks. Then I redid his black greasepaint and used a makeup brush to draw thin red whiskers on his face. "Much better. Now you're so the panther."

I finished with his face and looked up. Kim was staring over at us from the pumpkin table, her eyes narrowed. "Mine," she mouthed, pointing at Finn.

I put the makeup brush down and busied myself organizing the greasepaints.

Finn and I didn't talk much the rest of the day—or ever again. I pretty much ignored him. It didn't seem worth it. But even so, on the bus ride back he and Kim got in a whispered argument in the seat behind me and Nora.

"So thanks a lot," she hissed at him, as the bus pulled out of the parking lot.

"What?"

"You know."

"What?"

---

[2] Freddy Krueger is the insane serial killer from the *Nightmare on Elm Street* movies with knives on the ends of his fingers and a horrible, red-scarred face. He murders people by haunting their dreams, so no one is safe if they fall asleep.

"Finn, don't give me that."

"What?"

"If you don't know, I'm not telling you."

"Kim, please. Whatever it is, I'll make it up to you."

"You were ignoring me all afternoon."

"I was not!"

"Especially after you didn't come to dinner with my parents last night, I'd think you could bother to hang out with me in school."

"I had to work. There wasn't anything I could do."

"You could have got a sub."

Finn sighed. "I had to work because I need the money, Kim."[3]

"Fine. So ignore me all day, then. Just ignore me forever." And then, as we got off the bus and stepped into the Tate parking lot, she really let him have it. When Kim stops beating around the bush and says what she really thinks— look out. She let forth a string of obscenities in English and Japanese, and told him she never wanted to see him again. There was no reasoning with her. Once she's decided she's right and someone else is wrong, there's nothing anyone can do to change her mind. Everyone was standing around in the parking lot, listening and kind of pretending that they weren't. It was a real scene. Finally, Kim stormed off to the girls' bathroom and locked herself in a stall. Cricket and Nora and I went in there and tried to make her feel better, but she asked us to leave her alone, so we did.

---

[3] So Finn was probably on scholarship too. I had never realized that. Even though he worked at the B&O, it never really occurred to me that he *had* to.

93

The stud-muffin was in the doghouse for days after this—Kim called me that night and told me he had known about her parents' dinner party for weeks, and had said he would come, and when he didn't, all these annoying friends of her mother's had spent the evening asking where her mysterious vanishing boyfriend was, ha ha ha— and then he'd eaten lunch the next day with a bunch of soccer players, and if he wasn't going to pay attention to her and do stuff with her, why was he her boyfriend anyway and he could just go fuck himself.

I thought she was wrong, but I didn't say anything. She was my best friend. And three days later they were cuddling together in the library, so everything was okay.

When I got home that afternoon, my parents were in a fight. They were going to a costume party, and my mom wanted my dad to be a taco with her. She had spent the day at home, building a giant taco suit out of colored foam rubber, crepe paper and twine. She was going to be the filling, and my dad was supposed to be the shell.

"Elaine," he said, "I can't drive the car in a taco shell."

"Juana doesn't live that far," my mom countered. "You said you'd wear whatever I came up with."

"I didn't know it would be a *taco*," my dad complained.

"I spent all day on it. If you'd come in once from the deck, you'd have known what it was."

"It'll be too hot. I won't be able to sit down."

"You can put it in the trunk until we get there."

"I can't even move in this thing." My dad was wearing the foam rubber shell, his arms sticking out on either side. "How will I eat?"

"I'll feed you," said my mother.

"Very funny."

"It's romantic, Kevin. It's theatrical. Why can't you be a good sport about this?"

"It's a taco," he said. "It's not romantic."

"We'd be two parts of the same whole. I'll nestle in."

"Can't we wear the silly hats from last year?"

"Those are so boring!" my mom yelled. "Why are you always so conservative? Theater is my life! I'm a creative person! I can't go to the party in some silly hat. It's Halloween. All my friends will be there. Roo, you like the taco suit, don't you?"

"I'm staying out of this one," I said, flicking on the TV.

"Kevin, you're repressing my creativity!" my mom cried.

"No. I'm refusing to make a fool of myself and spend an evening sweating on my feet when I worked all afternoon in the garden."

"You shouldn't have spent all afternoon in the garden, then," my mom said, pouting.

"What was I supposed to do?" my dad yelled. "There's a frost predicted any day now!"

"You knew we were going out tonight."

"I'm ready to go out. I'm happy to go out. Just not in a taco shell!"

Blah blah blah. They went on for at least an hour.

My dad won.

My mom went off to take an angry shower. Then they squashed the foam rubber taco suit into two black plastic garbage bags and wore the silly hats to the party.

I called Jackson, and he came over, and we made out. I was still wearing my kitty-cat suit.

7. Chase (but it was all in his mind.)

The story of Chase Williams is important because it's a story about presents. That's what I figured out, when I talked about him with Doctor Z.

I don't see why boys can't give presents like normal people.[1] Kim got me this amazing red vintage jacket for my birthday last August. It fits just right. We all gave Nora a copy of *Playgirl* on Valentine's Day, since she wasn't going to have an actual valentine.[2] And last Christmas I got

---

[1] A massive, unfounded, sexist generalization, I know. Mr. Wallace would never let me get away with saying that.

But it's still how I feel.

[2] Kim bought it. She has a secret method for buying such things. She always gets tampons along with it, figuring the checkout clerk will be either too busy avoid-

my mother a book by a performance artist called Spalding Gray, which she read in less than a week. And Nora made me cupcakes the day after I won a 100-meter freestyle race (I usually place second or third—or I flat-out lose) and there were five of them, each with a squiggly letter in blue frosting: C-H-A-M-P.

These are good presents. Thoughtful. Some for special occasions, some just because. Normal, problem-free, everybody's happy.

But bring a boy into the picture, and the whole thing goes weird. Jackson and I had present-giving trouble, that's for sure.

●

After Hutch's gummy bears, the first present I ever got from a boy was an extremely pretty bead necklace from a boy named Chase Williams, who has since transferred to a different school.

He was an awkward boy. Downy black hair sprouted across his upper lip. His neck was short. Starting in seventh, everyone at Tate has to do a sport, and Chase and I were both swimmers, so I saw him several days a week at practice. But I didn't really know him. A completely typical conversation between us:

Him: "You doing freestyle?"

Me: "Uh-huh."

Him: "Me too."

---

ing looking her in the eye because of the tampons, or will assume that whatever it is—cigarettes, beer, *Playgirl*—is just part of a routine drugstore run and not anything she came in specially to buy.

Me: "Hundred or two hundred?"

Him: "Two."

Me: "Sounds good."

Him: "Yeah."

Me: "Well, I gotta get changed."

Him: "Okay. Later."

Chase mainly hung around with this other swimming guy, Josh, who was big and redheaded and laughed so loud you could hear him all the way inside the girls' locker room.

It was early December, almost time for the middle school Christmas dance.[3] One day, about an hour after practice, my phone rang. Josh.[4]

"What's up?" I asked. I couldn't think why he was calling me.[5]

"Chase wants to ask you something," he said.

I was thoroughly confused. "What?"

"Chase! Get on the phone!" Josh started giggling. I wanted to hang up, but that seemed rude, and no boy had

---

[3] Yes, Tate is that Christiancentric (as Mr. Wallace would say). They have a Christmas dance for the sixth, seventh and eighth graders every year. It's like they never even heard of Hanukkah or Kwanzaa or atheism or Buddhism.

[4] Everyone at Tate has everyone else's phone number. There's a directory we all get every September.

[5] Katarina and Ariel and Heidi were always talking about their phone conversations with boys. Already, in sixth grade. I'd think, How do they get started with these things? Do the boys just call them up for no reason? Or do they make an excuse, like Oh, I forgot the math homework? Or did the girls call the *boys?* I just can't picture any of the eleven-year-old boys we knew making phone calls on a regular basis.

ever called me on the phone before either, so I was kind of curious.[6] "Aw, he's gone in the other room. Hold on!" Josh put the phone down.

I sat there. This was so dumb. But I couldn't hang up, or I'd spend the rest of my life wondering what Chase had to say.[7]

"Ruby, are you there?" Josh's voice sounded breathless.

"Yeah."

"He wants to know—ow, Chase, that hurt!—he wants to know, do you want to go to the Christmas dance?"

"With him?" I *so* didn't. Chase was repulsive to me. I couldn't quite say why. But if I thought about slow-dancing with him, a creepy feeling went up my spine.

"She can tell me tomorrow!" yelled Chase in the background.

"Did you hear that?" asked Josh.

"She doesn't have to say right now!"

"Did you hear?"

"Yeah," I said. "All right. I'll think about it."

"She's thinking about it," Josh told Chase.

The next day, Josh came up to me as Kim and I were eating lunch. "This is from Chase," he said, pulling a bead necklace out of his pocket and scooting it toward me across the table. "For you."

---

[6] And once they were on the phone, what on earth did they talk about? At least with an IM, you can take a second to think about what you're going to write, figure out something to say.

[7] Not that any boys were IM-ing me in sixth grade, either. They definitely weren't. I just think I would have liked it better than phone calling, if they had.

The necklace was really pretty—but looking at it almost made me sick. I didn't want it. Taking it would feel like a promise. Like telling Chase there was a thing between us.

I didn't want a thing.

And why was Josh doing all the talking for him?[8]

I looked around the refectory, but I couldn't see Chase anywhere. "How come he's giving me this?" I asked.

Kim rolled her eyes. "Duh. He likes you."

"Yeah," said Josh. "I told you, he wants to know if you'll go to the dance with him."

Was the necklace supposed to convince me? Like, Oh, I didn't like him before, but now that there's jewelry involved, I want to go?

"You could just go as a friend if you want," said Josh.[9] "You could still have the necklace."[10]

If I took the necklace, only horror could result. For instance, I'd have this necklace, and this Christmas dance date—both without even talking to Chase himself. Next time I saw him, I'd have to go up and say thank you, and tell him whether we were going as "just friends" or as—what? What would you even say? As "regular"? As

---

[8] Kim's analysis, back then: Chase was just shy. Doctor Z's analysis, now: Josh was the one who liked me and Chase never had anything to do with it at all.(!!)

[9] This sounds desperate, don't you think? I mean, what idiot would still want to go to a dance with a person he really liked, when the person made it clear that the situation was only platonic and it was basically a pity date? You'd spend the whole evening feeling like a reject.

[10] Oh, my God! I'm that idiot! That is exactly what I did with Jackson and the Spring Fling! I am obviously a desperate reject, as you will soon find out, if you keep reading.

"boyfriend and girlfriend"? There wasn't even a normal way to say it! And then I'd have to wear the necklace, and people would know about it, and it would be like we were going out, which might be nice since I'd never had a boyfriend—except that he grossed me out.

The whole situation made me feel like I couldn't get enough air in my lungs.

"I can't go to the dance," I said. "My family's going out of town." (Completely untrue.)

"Oh. Okay. Wait one sec." Josh jumped up and ran out of the refectory for a minute, presumably to confer with Chase outside. Then he came back. "You can still have the necklace," he said. "If you want to go to McDonald's with him on Friday."

"I'm a vegetarian."

"You could order fries."

I didn't know what to do. If I said I was busy Friday, it seemed like he'd come up with some other day, or try to get me to keep the necklace anyhow. "I'm not allowed to go out with boys," I said. "Or take presents from them, or anything. My mom says." (Again, completely untrue.)

"Really?" Josh looked skeptical.

"She's completely not allowed," Kim cut in. "Her mom is psycho."

"You wouldn't have to tell," Josh said.

"Oh, she'd find out for sure," I lied. "She finds out everything."

For weeks after that, I ducked into doorways and behind bushes to avoid Chase. At swimming, I looked down at the ground and pretty much tried to be invisible. I felt like a jerk for lying, and I knew he probably knew it was a lie, and the whole thing was a horror.

He didn't let me off the hook, either, by finding a new girl to go to the Christmas dance with. He went alone, and I went with Kim and Nora, and he asked me to slow-dance, even after everything that happened.

That time, I actually had the courage to tell him no. Not that I was out of town (which I obviously wasn't), not that my parents wouldn't let me, not that I was a vegetarian. Just no.

Maybe it was because he had had the courage to ask me to my face.

●

On TV there are these diamond commercials: men buying women expensive gifts, and the women swooning with delight. Jackson and I used to make fun of those ads; we'd be sitting in the rec room at his house, watching TV, squashed together in one big armchair, and we'd laugh at how excited the ladies would get over a bit of shiny rock that doesn't even have a function. "Doesn't she want something more personal?" Jackson said, about one lady who started to cry when her husband gave her the twenty-fifth-anniversary diamond bracelet. "Doesn't she want something unique? I would never buy you some shiny rock that's just like a million other shiny rocks, given to a million other girls."

"What if I had a shiny rock collection?" I asked. "What if shiny rocks were my thing?"

"Then I'd go to the beach and find a rock myself, and shine it up with sandpaper and a chamois cloth," he said.

"Cheapskate," I laughed.

"It would be special," he said. "It would be different."

We had been going out for five weeks at that point, and the thing I didn't say was that a rock—even a rock shined up with a chamois cloth—really doesn't seem as nice to me as a diamond bracelet.

I mean, it's a friggin' rock.

Jackson didn't understand how to give me presents. You'd think something like that wouldn't matter between two people who are having lollipop taste tests and three-hour kissing sessions. But it did. Back in sixth grade, that necklace Chase tried to give me wasn't just a present. It was more like a bribe, or a plea for me to like him. And with Jackson, the things he gave me weren't just presents, either. They were apologies. Or halfhearted obligations. Or cover-ups.

Below, a list of present-giving misdemeanors, perpetrated by Jackson Clarke upon the unsuspecting and inexperienced Ruby Oliver.

One: In first month of going out, put a tiny ceramic frog in my mail cubby every Monday morning. There were four. I still have them on my desk. Each one is in a different position and has a different expression on its face. Okay, that's not a misdemeanor. It's very nice. But then—

Two: Stopped with the frogs. No explanation. That fifth Monday, I looked in my mail cubby first thing, all frog-ready, and it was empty.

I looked again after my first class, and it was still empty.

It was empty all day.

Why no frog?

I felt stupid bringing it up because it was just a tiny ceramic frog and not a big deal or anything, but I wondered all day why he hadn't given me a frog. Then I thought, Maybe he forgot to bring it to school with him and he'll bring it on Tuesday.

But on Tuesday, no frog, again! A frogless day.

At the end of Tuesday, Jackson asked me if anything was wrong. I tried to make a joke of it, felt so dumb even bringing it up, but it was bothering me, like we had this special thing that we did and now he'd canceled it. "Ruby!" he laughed. "There were only four frogs, that's why! They had four different expressions at the store, and I bought them all. I ran out. It doesn't mean anything."

I said okay, and I was sorry to be so silly. But if I had been him—that is, if I had been the one giving the frogs, I would have found a frog substitute for the Monday after the frogs ran out. I would have found a gummy frog, or a plastic frog bath toy, or written a note with a frog on it. At the very least, I would have warned him that the fourth frog was, in fact, the final frog. Something. He wouldn't have gone wondering and feeling disappointed for two days.

Three: Christmas. A reasonable time to give a present to your girlfriend, no?

Yes.

But Jackson's family went to Tokyo for the holidays, so he wasn't there on the actual day. The day before he left, I gave him this great brown leather coat I found at Zelda's

Closet for thirty dollars. It was from the seventies, I think, and he had been saying he wanted a jacket like that for months. I was so happy when I found it. And he completely liked it—but he didn't have anything for me.

"I'm sorry," he said. "I didn't know you were getting me anything."

I said it was okay, it didn't matter. But then, when he got back from Tokyo, I kind of thought he'd have something for me, then. Actually, I completely expected he'd have something. Is that insane? Bick bought Meghan a cashmere sweater. Finn saved up his money from working at the B&O and gave Kim a stack of CDs she'd been wanting. My dad gave my mom an amber necklace. But it was already January when Jackson got back, so I guess he figured Christmas was over and he had missed it.

Four: We had a fight. Jackson forgot that he had plans with me on Saturday, nothing much, he was just coming over to watch a movie on TV, but still. On Friday night we hung around at his friend Matt's place with a bunch of his friends, and when he dropped me off, he very clearly said, "See you tomorrow."

I called him on Saturday morning, and his mom said the Dodge needed a new muffler and he had taken his car to the shop and would be back around two. By five o'clock he hadn't called.

By six o'clock he hadn't called.

At seven, I called him again. "You just missed him," she said. "Matt came by and picked him up. I think they went to the game."

Well, I could go to the basketball game, if I wanted,

and see him there. But the bus to Tate takes like forty-five minutes and only comes once an hour, and my mom and dad had gone to Juana's house for a dinner party, so they weren't driving me anywhere. Besides, I didn't think any of my friends were going, and it seemed weird to go alone. I called Kim, and she was going to the circus with Finn; Nora and Cricket were over at Cricket's and said I could come meet them at the B&O for coffee at nine, but I thought maybe Jackson's mom was wrong and he was getting a ride to my house from Matt, not going to the basketball game at all. So I stayed home to wait for him.

He didn't come.

I rang Jackson's cell, but he didn't pick up.

Our house seems cold and overly quiet when it's empty. Because it's on the water.

I read a little and watched TV, and made myself some ramen.

It seems stupid, but by ten o'clock I was crying. I had dialed the cell three more times, but I didn't leave a message. Finally, I choked out the most relaxed-sounding thing I could think of to say, after the tone: "Hey, it's Ruby. I somehow thought we had plans tonight? I guess I was wrong. But give me a call."

He called at midnight. My parents weren't home yet. He said he had just gotten the message, and I sounded upset, what was up?

"I'm not upset," I said. "I thought you were coming over."

"I went to the game with Matt," he said. "It was excellent. Cabbie scored six times."

"Didn't you say you were coming over?" I asked.

"I don't think so, Roo."

"But you did," I said. "We talked about it last night. To watch *Annie Hall.*"

"We see each other all the time," Jackson said. "We see each other like every day."

"I know."

"So I need to go out with the guys sometimes, that's all."

"That's fine," I said. "I don't care. I just thought we had plans."

"It was a completely important game. We were playing Kingston."

"I was waiting for you."

He sighed. "Roo. Sometimes it's like you want me all to yourself."

"That's not it."

"Matt just came over and picked me up," he said. "He practically kidnapped me."

"Oh, so you *did* know we had plans?"

"He really wanted me to go; Kyle and the Whipper were in the back of the car. I swear, they pulled me in and wouldn't even let me get my coat."

"So you're saying you knew we had plans and you went to the game anyway? Without even calling?"

"I just forgot."

"Forgot to call, or forgot we had plans?"

"Ruby."

"What?"

"Why are you being so insecure?"

"I'm not insecure," I said—although I was. "I spent my Saturday night sitting home eating ramen, when I could have been *doing* something."

"Well, why didn't you do something? You could have gone to the game, or gone out with Nora. Or Cricket. Whatever."

"I didn't do anything because I had plans with you!" I cried.

There was a pause. "You're getting too worked up about this," Jackson said, finally.

I sniffed. I kind of hoped he could hear me crying over the phone and would realize what a jerk he'd been.

"Are you okay?" he finally said.

"Yeah." Although obviously I wasn't.

"You're being oversensitive, Roo," he said.

"Maybe."

"I just went to the game with some guys."

"That's not the point."

"It's not a big deal."

"Don't you want to know what the point was?"

"I got up at six for cross-country practice," Jackson said. "I'm completely shattered. We can talk about this tomorrow."

"Okay," I said. But I didn't hang up.

"I'm gonna go, now, Roo," he said.

"Okay, go, then."

"All right. I'm hanging up. Good night." And the line went dead.

The next day, Jackson called and came over in the afternoon. He brought me a brownie.

I ate it.

He said he was sorry. He should have called when he went to the game.

I thought he should have not gone to the game and should have come over to my house instead. But I didn't say anything about that.

I said the brownie was perfect, and brownies were my favorite, and did he feel like walking down the dock and looking at the boats? He said yes, and so we did.

But later, I wished I hadn't eaten that stupid brownie. I wished I had thrown it back at him and told him never to stand me up again.

Five: For Valentine's Day at Tate this year, the senior class decided to raise money for the Downtown Seattle Soup Kitchen by selling flowers and delivering them. For three weeks ahead of time, they took orders at a table in the main building: a dollar for a carnation, two dollars for a daisy, three for a rose. You'd put in an order, pay cash and write a note to go with the flowers. Then on February 14, the seniors delivered the bouquets; they were showing up in classrooms, at the refectory tables, in the hallways, calling out names.

A lot of girls had had the foresight to send each *other* flowers. It was worth a few dollars so that your girlfriend could have Bick or the Whipper or Billy Alexander or some other hot senior interrupt math class with a rose. So there were a lot of deliveries. I sent daisies to Kim and Cricket and Nora, and I sent Jackson six roses with an anonymous card—but of course it would still be obvious whom they were from.

When I got to school that day, the whole place was buzzing. Kim already had a dozen roses from Finn the stud-muffin, and there was a daisy from Cricket in my mail cubby with a funny note. I saw Jackson after third-period French, and he hadn't gotten the roses yet, so I didn't say anything. I got a rose from Kim and a daisy from Nora, and a carnation from this guy Noel who stood next to me in Painting Elective, with a long goofy poem about unrequited love.[11] Nora found the *Playgirl* in her mail cubby and cracked up.

Jackson sat with his friends at lunch, and I felt weird about him not having gotten the roses yet, so I pretended not to see him and hung out with Cricket, Kim and Nora. In fifth period, Nora showed me a rose she got from some guy she knew from basketball, which made her feel good even though she didn't like him "that way," and then asked to see what Jackson had sent me. I said Nothing yet, and she said, "Oh dear. I hope it's not a frogless day!"

"It better not be," I said—but I had a sinking feeling that wouldn't go away all through Biology/Sex Ed.

After, when I was crossing the quad to H&P, I ran into Jackson holding the roses I'd sent him. He kissed me and said, "These are from you, right?" and I thought, Who on

---

[11] In Painting Elective, we had been given this ridiculous assignment where we had to "convey the essence of the poem 'How Do I Love Thee? Let Me Count the Ways,'" and most people painted hearts and flowers and sunsets, but Noel painted a car wreck, working off a photo he had from a newspaper, and I painted a frog. Anyway, the poem he sent me started, "How do I love thee? As much as this carnation is worth (a dollar). As high as a pig can fly." And so on. So it wasn't serious.

earth else does he think it could be? Shouldn't he *know* they're from me?–but all I said was "Maybe," because I was trying to be mysterious, especially if he hadn't sent me anything.

In Mr. Wallace's class, now it was Cricket asking if I had anything yet, and when I said no, she said, "Don't worry. I hear it's a special order."

I couldn't think what a special order would be, but it sounded good, so I relaxed. Cricket had a rose from Pete, who's her boyfriend now, but she'd only just started liking him then. The Whipper delivered daisies to Kim, from a freshman who had a crush on her. A thousand hundred people asked me what I had from Jackson, and Heidi even advised me not to let him take me for granted, giving me this knowing look as if she knew him and all his tendencies a hundred times better than I did.

It wasn't like I had any control over whether he took me for granted or not, anyway. What was I supposed to do? Act like I didn't like him? He had been my boyfriend for six months already.

Finally, in seventh period, Billy Alexander interrupted Brit Lit with a delivery for me.

It was half a carnation.

Literally, a sad-looking white carnation sliced in half, with a note that said: "I would never buy you regular roses, like a million other roses given to a million other girls. Happy Valentine's Day. Jackson."

I tried to act pleased, but I could barely keep from crying. As soon as I got out the door of the classroom, I burst into tears. Kim was right there. "It's not even a rose," I cried, "it's the cheapest thing he could buy. It's only half of the cheapest thing he could buy."

"Oh, Roo," she said, "it's nice. It's unusual."

"It's soggy," I sniffed. "The card doesn't even say Love on it. People have been asking me all day and now all I've got is this soggy, ripped-up flower."

"I'm sure he thought you'd like it," Kim said. "He had to order it special."

"I'd rather have roses." I kept my head down so people walking down the hall wouldn't see I was crying.

"You want some of mine?" Kim asked.

"No," I wailed. "That's not it. I wanted something romantic."

"I'm sure he meant well." Kim patted my shoulder.

I ran out of school and found Meghan's Jeep in the parking lot. I didn't have an eighth-period class, but she did. She wouldn't come out to drive me home for another fifty minutes. I sat down on my backpack, leaning against a tire, and waited. Finally she came out, jangling her keys, wearing a new pair of running shoes (from Bick) and carrying two dozen red roses. I'm sure she noticed my face was all red and swollen, but she didn't ask any questions. We drove home in silence.

When I talked to him later, I just told Jackson "Thank you" for the flower.

"Why did you pretend you weren't upset?" asked Doctor Z.

"I didn't want to seem like it was important."

"Why not?"

"He'd say I was oversensitive. Or he'd think I didn't understand him, since I didn't like his present. Because he was being unique."

"Maybe *he* didn't understand *you.*"

"What?"

"Maybe Jackson didn't understand you. What you needed on Valentine's Day."

"It's a stupid holiday," I said.

●

When we got home from the appointment with Doctor Z, John Hutchinson (aka Hutch) was drinking pop on our front deck.

That's right. Hutch. Boy #3. On my deck.

My dad was next to him, beaming. "John, you know Roo!" he cried. "Here she is!"

"Hey there, Hutch," I said. What on earth was he doing at my house?

"Hey, Roo."

"Hutch! Is that what the kids call you?" My dad punched him on the arm playfully, all man to man.

"Nah." Hutch shrugged. "My friends call me John."

What friends?

"How come you're here?" I asked.

"John answered my ad for a carpentry and garden assistant," my dad said. "I put a flyer on the Tate bulletin board. You know, I'm greenhousing the southern deck?"

I knew. It had been my dad's dream to turn our southern deck into a tiny greenhouse, so his beloved plants wouldn't die over the winter, and so he could grow some exotica that would die in typical Seattle weather. He had been arguing with my mom about it for two years. She wanted him to relax and hang out with her on weekends, and use our savings for a family vacation. He wanted to spend the money and the weekends building the greenhouse.

"John's a plant man," my dad enthused. "He wants to be a botanist. But he's handy with a table saw, too, aren't you? And I'm going to teach him everything I know." My dad is never happier than when he's building something.

Hutch smiled and showed his gray, heavy-metal teeth. "Great houseboat," he said. "I never knew you lived in one of these."

Since when did he want to be a botanist? What was that yellowy stain on his KISS T-shirt? Why didn't he do something about his skin? I couldn't believe he was going to end up being the second boy ever to come over to my house and see my bedroom. "Why in the world *would* you know where I lived?" I snapped.

I didn't wait for a reply. I went inside and slammed the door.

I threw myself on the couch and turned on the TV, but I could hear my parents talking outside. "Don't mind Roo," Mom was saying. "Her boyfriend dropped her and she's been mopey ever since it happened. Full of anxiety."

"It's not about you," my dad added. "She's working through a lot of pain and forgiveness issues."

"And expressing a little adolescent rage," my mom said. "Kevin, I think we should actually be pleased to see Ruby expressing her anger openly. Don't you think that shows progress? She turns everything in on herself, John. She doesn't talk freely about her emotions. But she's seeing a therapist, and we're hoping that will help."

"Uh-huh," Hutch mumbled.

"Maybe that's normal for people your age," my mom went on. "What do you think?"

At that point, I went into the bathroom, took a long hot shower and tried to pretend none of them existed.

8. Sky (but he had someone else.)

Doctor Z thinks I have panic attacks because I don't express myself. Like I'm repressing how I really feel, and all this repression triggers anxiety. Blah blah blah.

To take it out of therapy-speak, Doctor Z thinks I'm lying way too much of the time. She thinks I lie to my parents. She thinks I lied to Jackson.

She thinks I lie to myself, mainly. Not about truths or facts. About feelings.

And all that lying makes me not be able to breathe, because the horror that's inside me pretty much *has* to express itself somehow, so it starts my heart up like a jackhammer and turns off my lungs.

I never thought of myself as someone who lies at all.

Actually, I think I'm pretty truthful. But maybe she was right. "How can I be honest with anyone when everyone is lying to *me*?" I said to Doctor Z.

"Who's lying to you?"

"Jackson."

"Who else?"

"Kim."

"Who else?"

I felt like there were hundreds of people. But I couldn't think of anyone.

We were silent.

"Who is it that *you're* not honest with?" asked Doctor Z.

"No one."

"No one?"

"I'm not a liar."

118

"I'm asking if there are times when you don't tell the truth about how you feel."

"I'm not a liar."

"Ruby, that's not what I asked you. I asked if you were honest about your feelings."

Ag. Therapy is such a pain in the ass. I told her I wanted to change the subject and talked about how annoying my mother was for the rest of the hour.[1] But then I went home and I made a list of all the lies I told to Jackson.

---

[1] Seriously, seriously annoying—and it wasn't getting any better. In February, she went macrobiotic, and ever since then had been running around our kitchen chopping tofu and steaming brown rice and talking about how the green top leaves of the carrot were good for the top of the body and the orange root of the carrot was good for the lower half of the body.

Dinner at our house became entirely inedible. There I'd be, stirring a mess of

1. I didn't mind that he never came to my swim meets.
2. Watching the cross-country team run was interesting.
3. Japanese anime movies were interesting.
4. I liked his friend Matt.
5. I liked the half carnation.
6. I liked his new haircut.
7. I liked his mom.
8. I didn't mind the frogs ending.
9. I didn't mind him playing tennis with Heidi.
10. I didn't mind when he said he'd call, but then forgot.
11. I didn't mind him making friends with Kim.

When I got to eleven, I realized I could very easily get to twenty. Or thirty. Or forty. I put my pen down.

I was obviously a big huge liar and didn't even know it.[2]

I actually never thought of myself as lying to Jackson.

---

tofu and carrot around and wishing for French fries—or at least spaghetti with pesto sauce, like we used to have—and my mother would get on my case about whether I hated my thighs and thought I was fat, because it seemed neurotic to her that I wasn't eating this perfectly good dinner, and "Kevin, did you notice that Roo isn't eating, and maybe she's getting anorexic?"

Later, when she was on the phone or had gone to bed, my dad and I would sit together and eat bowls of breakfast cereal, we were so hungry.

[2] What about this Sky character whose name is at the front of the chapter, you are wondering?

Sky was the first boy who really seemed to like me, and I liked him back. I met him at a swim meet (he went to Saint Augustine's) and I gave him my e-mail. He started sending me a lot of instant messages, funny jokes and flirtatious questions, like what movie star would I want to have babies with. He asked me out to pizza, and my dad drove me in to the University District and dropped me off. It

Well, some of them were lies I told to make him feel good. The haircut. His mom. But most of the others are actually lies that I told *myself*, and didn't even know were lies, until I made that list. I would be bored watching cross-country, but I'd somehow tell myself I was learning about the sport. I hated the Japanese animation films he always wanted to rent, but I told myself I was getting a taste for them. His friend Matt isn't awful, just kind of lunkheaded and boring—but I spent time with him every single week, and never stopped to think that I'd rather not. If Jackson asked him along with us, I never objected.

Jackson made friends with Kim around Thanksgiving. He and I went over to her house the morning of the holiday, and we all sat on her front porch, shucking corn and peeling apples for Mae Yamamoto, who seemed to view us as hired labor.

We were joking around and talking about Madame Long, the French teacher, and how she collected stuffed pigs, and how does one get started collecting such a thing? And Jackson said something to Kim in Japanese.

She said something back.

Then him.

Then her.

---

was pretty fun. We got jumbo-size Cokes and played Ms. Pac-Man on the machine in the foyer. He held my hand afterward. But the next day I saw him in the mall with his arm around another girl. I asked around and found out he had had the same girlfriend for like three months.

I sent him an IM: "Do you have a girlfriend?"

He wrote back: "Not yet, but I'm hoping! Do you have a boyfriend?"

I switched off the computer and never talked to him again.

Liar.

I shucked corn.

Kim squeezed my knee. "You didn't tell me Jackson was fluent!"

"He was in Tokyo for a year," I said.

"Really?" cried Kim, although I know she knew already. "I'm applying to go on an exchange program. Where were you hanging out?"

More Japanese going on. Back and forth. "Sorry, Roo," they both said, at one time or another.

And I shucked corn.

From then on, they were friends. They did things together and talked on the phone. Jackson was a big proponent of boy/girl friendship, which in theory I appreciated. Yes! It's important to be friends with the opposite sex, I thought. I was friends with Noel, wasn't I? We should all be comfortable with everyone, and we shouldn't be jealous and possessive, and it's good for boys and girls to hang out together and not only see each other as sexual objects.

But I did feel strange when I saw Kim's handwriting on a note, half in Japanese and half in English, sticking out of Jackson's back pocket. Or the one time he left my house on Sunday afternoon and I found out the next day he'd gone over to her place after, to study for a test in the Asian History Elective they were both taking. Or the time he was taking me to a restaurant to eat Japanese food for the first time, and he invited Kim to come too, without even checking with me. It turned out we had a great time, but I was also a little disappointed because Jackson and I had never gone out to eat anywhere fancy before, and I had dressed up for a romantic date.

Not once did the two of them flirt in front of me.

No extra smiles, no longing looks, no secret jokes.

Never did Jackson talk about Kim being pretty. Never did Kim change how she acted when I told her stuff about Jackson. She knew every detail of what went on, and the only thing she ever said was that she knew he liked me and that his intentions were good—the way she did when I was upset about the half carnation. Never did Jackson stop kissing me the way he kissed me, like it mattered hugely, putting his hands on my face. Never did he stop coming over to my house, rooting around in our (macrobiotic) refrigerator, pulling me into my bedroom the minute my parents went outside on the deck so we could make out on the bed and feel the warm bare skin up each other's shirts.

When I called, he always said, "Oh, I'm glad it's you."

When we watched a movie, he always held my hand.

He still put notes in my mail cubby almost every day, with jokes and little stories about stuff he'd been thinking about.[3]

---

[3] "Roo. The old parental units were gravely disappointed you weren't able to attend our wondrous chili feast. Although we were all somewhat remorseful, the chili did flow, and how! It went round and round and was consumed with grunting and smacking sounds of delight, until all that remained was a bowl containing an amount of chili that would be disgraceful to give to a pygmy shrew as an after-dinner snack. Missed you. Jackson."

And: "I am writing this at Kyle's house. We are d-r-u-n-k because his mom gave us wine at dinner. Trivia: Guess who has a toothbrush that permanently lives at Kyle's house? Answer: Me, silly! Good night, good night, from your woozy, bad-handwritin' man, Jackson."

I can't throw them out, somehow. I know I should.

He was my boyfriend, I was his girlfriend. Whatever else went wrong, that seemed completely clear.

Until seven days before the Spring Fling dance.

Friday night, Jackson and I went to a movie. He didn't reach over and hold my hand, like usual, but when I reached over to take his, he stroked my palm. After, we got ice cream at a place in the mall, but the lights were fluorescent-bright and the movie had been something sad with people dying in it, and somehow the mood was dead. Neither of us talked too much.

He dropped me off at the edge of our dock without coming in, though we kissed for a long time and even got in the backseat of the car so we could lie down.

The next morning, he called around eleven. "Roo, we have to talk."[4]

"What about?" I asked.

"Not on the phone."

"Want to come over?"

"I can't come till after the ball game. Matt and Kyle are due here any minute to watch it on TV."

"Okay. What do you want to talk about?"

"Can I just come over at six?"

"Sure. Are you staying for dinner?"

"I can't. I have something to do at seven."

"What?"

"Um. This thing with my mom."

"Okay. What is this about?"

123

[4] It is so mean to tell someone you "need to talk" but then refuse to say what about. If you ever want to dump someone, or even just tell the person something important, don't go saying you "need to talk." Just talk and be done with it.

Jackson paused. "I'll see you at six, Ruby. We can talk then."

Any idiot would probably know he was going to break up with me, and part of me knew it too. What else does "We have to talk" mean? and why else would he come all the way over to my house when he had to be somewhere else an hour later? But the Spring Fling was coming up, this big event Tate has every year on a miniyacht, and I had saved my money and bought a vintage dress from the 1970s. Jackson was taking me out for dinner and then to the dance. Afterward, a bunch of kids were actually coming over to my place to hang out, since the dock for the miniyacht was a short way over from our houseboat.

So it didn't seem like we could possibly be breaking up. Things were happening. We had plans. We were together.

But even with all that, the day was like torture. I called Kim six times.

She was out. Her cell was off. I figured she was with Finn. I left messages, and she didn't ring back.

I called Nora. "It must be sex," she said. "You were lying down in the car together last night, now he's all overexcited. He wants to go all the way. Or at least to third base."

I called Cricket. "It must be the whole spending-time-with-the guys-thing. He needs to go out and do manly things with his manly man friends. Pete's like that. Did I tell you what he said to me last night?" And then blah blah on about Pete and his adorable machismo.

I tried not to deal with my parents. It was a pretty day,

so I took my homework out to the end of our dock and did it out there. I was reading *Great Expectations* for Brit Lit. Then I went back into the house and used my dad's computer to write up my science lab for Bio/Sex Ed. Then I took a long shower and blew out my hair and put on makeup and my favorite jeans and tried on six shirts. My stomach was sticking out, all of a sudden, and everything I wore looked funny. I tried a different bra. I took the makeup off. I put some of it back on. I put on perfume and it smelled like too much. Finally I put on my old swim team sweatshirt and figured at least it would look like I didn't care what I was wearing.

Jackson was on time. He looked gorgeous, his hair curling at the back of his neck and an old T-shirt untucked at the waist. He came in and made small talk with my father for ten minutes. Then he asked if I wanted to take a walk down the dock.

I had just spent most of the day down at the end of it, but I said okay.

When we got there, he broke up with me. Only, he kept saying it like I wanted it, too.

"We haven't been getting along," he said. "We want different things."

"I don't think I'm the one for you," he said. "I don't think I make you happy."

"We need time to think things over," he said. "You need someone different from me."

This is Jackson Clarke, I thought, who used to really like me.

This is Jackson Clarke, who used to be mine.

This is Jackson Clarke, who kissed me *last night*.

This is Jackson Clarke.

This is Jackson Clarke.

This is Jackson Clarke.

"Why?" I asked him.

"It's not your fault," he said. "We just need to think it out."

"Was there something I did?"

"Of course not. Don't be so sensitive."

"You're breaking up with me and you want me not to be sensitive?"

"You blow things up, Roo. I'm not breaking up with you. It's not like that. I'm just saying we should have some time apart. We both know that's true."[5] He looked at his watch. "I gotta go. I have to be at that thing at seven. I'm sorry."

I sniffed. "Can't you call and be late?"

"I really can't," he said.

"Why not?"

He didn't answer. "We'll be friends, right?"

I nodded.

"That would mean a lot to me. I do like you, Roo."[6]

---

[5] What was he saying? Were we breaking up, or not? The vagueness made the whole thing even worse than it already was.

[6] The next day, Nora pointed out to me that this is a trend. The breaker-upper always says that he wants to be friends, and tries to get the break-upee to commit to undying friendship immediately after he has just made her feel like she wants to crawl into a hole and die. I guess he asks so he doesn't feel guilty. And the girl says yes, because it's a little less like being broken up with, if the boy still wants the connection of being friends.

He kissed me quickly on the cheek, and stood up to leave.

I started to cry.

He was already walking up the dock. I heard his car door slam. The engine turned over, and he drove away.

●

I called Kim three more times that night, but I couldn't reach her. Cricket and Nora had gone to the movies, but at nine o'clock they answered Nora's cell together. "Oh, sweetie, I'm sorry," said Nora, over and over, but she kept interrupting everything I was saying to explain the situation to Cricket, who was sitting right next to her saying "What? What is it?" all the time.

"I'd kill Pete if he ever did that to me," said Cricket, when she finally grabbed the phone. "Did I tell you what he said about the Spring Fling?" Then we lost the connection because they were in Nora's dad's car and he was driving over the bridge.

●

I told my parents about the breakup on Sunday at dinner. I had to explain because my mom asked why my eyes were all puffy.

Mom: "Oh, I never liked him anyway. He's a horrible boy.

Dad: "Elaine, she needs to come to a place of forgiveness. Otherwise she'll never move on."

Mom: "It just happened. She needs to vent. She needs to express her anger."

Me: "Mom, I–"

Mom: "Roo, be quiet. She needs to raise her voice and be heard!"

Dad: "I wonder how Jackson is feeling right now. Roo, can you think about his perspective, come to an understanding of his position? Because that's the way you'll truly transcend the negativity of this experience."

Mom: "I never liked the way he'd honk the horn for you without coming in."

Monday at school, I felt lost. The beat of every day had been Jackson. Early morning, he'd be in the refectory drinking tea. After third period, quick kiss in the main hallway. We'd usually eat lunch together; I'd see him crossing the quad after fifth; and he'd be waiting for me after lacrosse practice (swim season is over). Now, I spent the day half avoiding him and half hoping he'd see me in one of our usual spots and have a change of heart. But when I finally did see him in the refectory at lunch, he was sitting with Matt and a bunch of the guys. "Hey, Roo," he said, "what's up?"—and turned away, before I could even answer.

Kim was shocked and sweet when I saw her in first period and finally told her what had happened, although she said a few things that in retrospect seem evil: "You were kind of expecting it, though, weren't you?"

No.

"But things had been getting weird for a while."

"I don't know what happened," I said. "It's like he turned a switch off inside himself. Just since Friday. He liked me on Friday, and on Saturday he didn't care."

"You'll be happier without him, though," said Kim,

patting my arm. "If you ask me, he was never the one for you."

"What do you mean?"

"You two are mismatched," said Kim. "It wasn't going to work out."

"Mismatched how?"

"You know, you want different things," she said.

"Like what? Was he talking to you about me?"

"No, that's not it," said Kim. "I'm trying to cheer you up, Roo."

"I can't be cheered up," I said.

"Sorry."

"I don't mean to snap at you," I said. "It's just the most frogless of all frogless days."

"Let me buy you an ice cream," she said, putting her arm around me. And she did. I had a toasted almond from the refectory, right after first period.

●

That was on Monday. That afternoon I went over to Cricket's and we all made chocolate chip cookies and ate them with our feet in the hot tub. Tuesday was the same living hell as Monday, only it was clear the entire school knew that Jackson had broken up with me, and people like Katarina and Ariel said, "Ruby, how are you feeling?" in a know-it-all sympathetic way, and people like Matt and Kyle said "Hey" in the hallway but didn't stop to talk like they used to.

Tuesday after lacrosse I went with Cricket and Nora to the B&O. Kim didn't want to come; she said she had a lot of homework.

Finn Murphy was there behind the counter. He was moping around, like a muffin with all the blueberries picked out, Cricket said. Finally, he came over to our table and sat down for a minute. Hey, what was Kim up to? he wanted to know. Where was she? Did we know whether she'd been busy lately, or something?

She wasn't picking up her cell. He actually hadn't seen her all weekend.

None of us knew, but when he left to go back to work behind the counter we concluded that Kim had definitely lost interest in the stud-muffin. Poor little muffin. Mini-muffin. Mopey muffin. We left him a big tip and a funny note on a paper napkin.

Wednesday morning, Kim announced she'd broken up with Finn. He wasn't "the one," and she felt like she was wasting her time. She was a little shattered, though, she said. He was such a nice guy.

The rest of the day was normal, aside from my broken heart.

Wednesday night, Kim called me at home. "Roo, I wanted you to hear it from me," she said.

"Hear what?" She had called during dinner. My mother and father were eating steamed mushrooms, tofu and brown rice, listening to every word I was saying.

"Please don't be mad."

"I won't," I said. I couldn't imagine what I'd be mad about.

"Promise?"

"Okay, okay. What is it?"

A pause. "Jackson and I are going out now."

I couldn't even say anything. I just breathed into the phone.

"We're such good friends," she said. "He was talking to me about all the problems you two were having, trying to work stuff out, and that brought us really close together."

"What problems?" I didn't even know Jackson thought we had problems.

"It wasn't like he was saying anything bad," said Kim. "It was like he needed support. He needed someone who'd be there for him."

"I wasn't there for him?"

"Please, Ruby," Kim said. "Don't be too upset. It just happened. We didn't mean it to. And I'd never do this to you, except the thing with you was never working out anyway—and I really think Jackson and me are meant to be."

131

"What do you mean, never working out anyway?"

"Well, not for a long time between you two," she said. "You know that as well as I do."

"When did it start?" I asked.

"Only yesterday, I swear. We never acted on our feelings before. I hope you'll believe me about that. I wanted you to be the first to know."

"Um-hum."

(Never acted on them *before*? How long had this been going on?)

"Please don't be mad. It's not like we could even help it. It's like fate."

"Um-hum." My parents were eyeballing me now, tilting their heads as if to say, "This is family dinnertime, could you get back to the table?"

"Really," said Kim. "I've never felt like this before. I think he's the one. He's like Tommy Hazard."

"Why were you guys talking about me?" I asked.

"Jackson meant well, Roo, you have to believe that. He's not the kind of guy to ever cheat on anyone. He needed an ear, he was so confused."

"I gotta go," I said.

"Please don't be mad," she said. "When you find your Tommy Hazard, you'll understand. I honestly couldn't help it."

I hung up the phone.

That night, I had my first panic attack, in the bathroom while I was brushing my teeth. I felt hot, and then cold. I was sweating and when I put my hand on my chest I could feel my heart thumping like it was going to leap out of my skin. I lay down on the floor in my pajamas and looked at the ceiling and tried to breathe. There were black mildew spots up there I had never noticed.

9. Michael (but I so didn't want to.)

You might count Michael Malone as my first kiss. Technically, maybe, he was.

But officially, he wasn't at all.

Everyone else I've ever heard of had kissed at least *someone* by the end of seventh grade.[1] But not me. Then the

---

[1] Well, except for Finn Murphy. Kim was his first—and he was *fifteen* when that happened.

"You devirginized him!" shouted Cricket, when Kim told us about Finn, back in October.

"He started it," Kim giggled. "It wasn't *me* doing anything to *him*."

"But you were his first! He'll remember you his whole life," laughed Cricket. "Blueberry's first kiss."

"Was he good?" Nora wanted to know.

"Hey," interrupted Cricket. "If he doesn't know how to kiss yet, I can help

summer after seventh, I went back to Camp Rainier, the same camp where I had dreamt about Ben Moi for four straight weeks—only this year, instead of singing and going on nature hikes and doing crafts projects with yarn, all anybody did was play Spin the Bottle.[2] Girls Twelve/Thirteen was right next door to Boys Twelve/Thirteen, and after lights-out, we'd grab a flashlight and troop over to a

---

you. Because Kaleb was like the worst kisser ever. He slobbered all over me and stuck his tongue in way too far."

"Gross. What did you do?" I asked.

"I trained him!" giggled Cricket. "Only I didn't complete the program because he dumped me before I could finish."

"What was the training?"

"Oh, it was a whole regime," said Cricket. "Kissing boot camp."

"Did you tell him he was a bad kisser?"

"No. You have to be subtle. Like, I held on to his head to prevent him jamming his tongue down my throat, grabbing his ears almost. And I tried to kiss him lying down on a couch, so I could be on top. You get a lot less slobber that way."

"Oh, my god, he must have been awful," said Nora.

"You cannot imagine the horror." Cricket rolled her eyes dramatically.

"What else?"

"I kissed his neck a lot, but you can't go on like that forever. Eventually the lips have to get involved."

"What else?"

"I can't tell you," snickered Cricket. "It's private. Anyway, I want to hear about the stud-muffin."

"Oh, he was good right out of the starting gate," said Nora. "We know that already."

"Is that true?" I asked Kim.

Kim nodded with a smug, happy look on her face. "No training required. He's a natural talent."

[2] I exaggerate, of course. We went on hikes and did plenty of yarn projects. What I mean is, all we thought about was Spin the Bottle. No one cared about Capture the Flag, or the Rainier Mountain Singers, or woodland safety, or anything else we had been interested in the year before.

woodsy clearing a short way off. The boys would all be wearing jeans and T-shirts (what did they sleep in, I wondered?), but we girls would go in our nightgowns, because it seemed cuter and more adventurous. Plus, it was too much bother to change.

Ben Moi wasn't at camp, much to the disappointment of nearly every girl who'd been there the previous summer. But there was a pack of reasonably interesting, if woefully short, boys—maybe eight who showed up for Spin the Bottle on a regular basis. And twelve of us girls.[3] The way the game worked was this:[4]

Everyone sat in a circle. In the middle was an empty plastic pop bottle, resting on a big atlas someone had borrowed from the camp's small library of nature-related books. A boy would spin the bottle, and when it came to rest, it would be pointing at a girl. If it pointed at a boy, he got a redo. Sometimes, if he didn't want the girl he got, he'd claim it was pointing at a boy sitting next to her, and redo. Or the bottle would skid off the atlas, and he'd redo. Or, he wouldn't get a good spin, and he'd redo. Or, the girl he got would claim there was some kind of technicality that made his spin invalid (because she didn't want to kiss him), and he'd have to redo.

---

[3] What were the non–Spin the Bottle boys *doing?* Were they just not *interested*? Were they totally invulnerable to peer pressure? And why does it seem like there are always more girls than boys in these situations? Girls are always having to dance with each other, or they like the same boy, or they went out with the same boy. Just once, I'd like to see a situation where there were *too many boys*.

[4] Oh. That situation with too many boys? I *have* seen it. It was my actual *life* at the end of sophomore year. And it was not pretty.

Be careful what you wish for, because getting it can be a complete debacle.

Most of the game was taken up with redos. When the bottle finally pointed at a girl, and everyone agreed it was official, the couple would go off a short ways into the dark woods and have "Seven Minutes in Heaven."[5] While they were doing this, the rule was that everyone had to stay seated in the circle—but we all tried as hard as we could to see what was going on out there, and anyone who *could* see anything would report back to everyone else in a loud voice.

Then the couple would come back to the circle, sometimes holding hands, and then it would be the next boy's turn.

The only girls in our cabin who didn't go on these moonlit adventures were a skinny girl who rocked back and forth in her chair and mumbled things to herself, a fourteen-year-old who was completely angry at being in the Twelve/Thirteen cabin and wouldn't speak to any of us and a girl who spent all her time reading books like *Misty of Chincoteague* and talking about how she wished she was at horse camp instead.

I pretty much had to play, to avoid becoming a leper, but I was terrified. I had no idea what people were doing during the Seven Minutes. Kissing, I figured, but seven minutes was a really long time (we had a stopwatch) and how long could you kiss for? Would you stand up, or sit

---

[5] At the camp Kim and Nora went to ("too expensive," said my father; "too establishment," said my mother), these were two separate games. Spin the Bottle was just for kissing, and you did it right in front of everyone. And Seven Minutes in Heaven started with people picking names out of a hat and then they went into a closet for the seven minutes. So not only did I have my first kiss with Michael Malone, who grossed me out—if we had been playing the game right, it never would have happened.

down on a log or something? Would you hug? If so, where would you put your hands? And I had boobs, but I didn't normally wear a bra under my nightgown, and what if the boy tried to feel my boobs with no bra? Would he think that was weird? Or would he think it was weird if I *was* wearing a bra underneath my nightgown? Plus, I had good reasons not to want to kiss *any* of the boys we played Spin the Bottle with. Two of them were obnoxious. Three were physically repulsive. One was cute but extremely short, and I couldn't figure out how it would work if I had to kiss him because he'd have to stand on tiptoe. That left two acceptably cute boys—but one of them my friend Gracia liked (so he was off-limits), and the other had called me four-eyes (so I knew he didn't want to kiss me).

For the first week of camp, I managed to avoid kissing anybody by claiming a redo every time a bottle pointed to me. Then, I begged Gracia to help me by claiming redos or saying the bottle was pointing at someone else. She agreed, and I stayed unkissed—until the third week, when I told some other girls about how Gracia had failed the pencil test, where you stick a pencil under your boob and see if the fold of your boob will hold it up. You fail if the pencil stays.[6]

Gracia's boobs were big, and her pencil stayed, and of course she was furious that I told everyone.[7] But instead of

---

[6] I completely fail the pencil test, now. My pencil stays right up there, tucked beneath my boob. But that summer, my chest was only just starting to grow, so my pencil fell on the floor.

[7] I wonder if I should look her up on the Internet and send her an e-mail: "Dear Gracia Rodriguez. I am sorry I told everyone about you and the pencil test. My own boobs are now saggy and I feel your pain. I never should have done it. Please forgive me, Ruby Oliver."

yelling, she just contradicted me when I claimed a redo that night.

"Roo, it's pointing right at you," she said. "Why are you always saying redos? Are you scared or something?"

"No," I said. "But look at the bottle. It's practically off the atlas."

"It's still pointing at you," Gracia said loudly.

Everyone looked at Michael Malone, one of the three physically repulsive boys, and the current spinner of the bottle. Michael shrugged. "It seemed like a decent spin to me," he said.

"Oooh, ooh, Michael and Roo!" someone chanted from the other side of the circle.

"Oooh, ooh, Michael and Roo!" some others echoed back.

"Go on, Ruby," said Gracia, bitterly. "Don't be such a baby."

"Oooh, ooh, Michael and Roo!"

This Malone character was probably a perfectly acceptable physical specimen to some people. I mean, I'm a perfectly acceptable physical specimen, but I know I grossed out that boy who called me four-eyes, plus Adam Cox, and probably a number of other people I don't even know about. It's just a matter of taste, and I'm sure he was a decent-looking boy by objective standards. But he disgusted me in the following ways:

1. He had too much saliva and always seemed to be sucking it back before it spilled out of his mouth accidentally.

2. His legs were quite hairy already, and his knee, cov-

ered with black hair, would stick out of a hole in his jeans. It looked like a dead animal.

3. He had pimples, which I didn't much mind on lots of kids, but he had some on the back of his neck that bothered me.

4. His nose turned up at the front in a way that I know a lot of the girls thought was cute, but frankly, I found it piggy.

I walked into the depths of the dark forest with this piggy, dead-animal, pimply saliva boy.

"Oooh, oooh! Michael and Roo!"

We got to a big tree and Michael ducked behind it.

"Oooh, oooh! Michael and Roo!"

I knew everyone could see me through the dark in my white nightgown, so I stepped behind the tree as well, staying as far away from Michael as I could manage. He put his big, cold hand on my shoulder, puckered up and pushed his lips against mine, waggling his head around, like in the movies.

I waggled my head back.

Our mouths weren't even open, and there was too much spit.

I didn't want to touch his pimply neck, so I put my hands on the outside edge of his shoulders. He smelled okay, like toothpaste, but when I opened my eyes for a second I saw that big piggy nose right next to my face.

Basically, it was like going to the dentist. Something unpleasant was happening around my mouth, someone else's face was too close to mine, and the best thing to do was to shut my eyes, breathe through my nose and think about something else. Was my mother sending me a care package? Would she remember I didn't like potato chips with ridges in them? What color would I glaze my pottery mug in arts and crafts tomorrow?

After what seemed like seven hours, someone yelled, "Time's up!" and Michael pulled away. "You're a good kisser," he whispered, and I felt relieved, even though when I thought about it I knew it couldn't possibly be true because I had been thinking about pottery and potato chips, waggling my head occasionally and wishing it was over. But at least he wouldn't go telling his friends I was disgusting.

I managed to get out of playing Spin the Bottle after that. With Gracia mad at me, I became a bit of a leper anyway, so the pressure was off. The next night, I said I was tired, and nobody yanked me out of bed and made me go.

I avoided looking Michael in the eye, worked on my pottery and counted the days (ten) until I could go home.

I didn't kiss anyone else for a year and a half.

●

I was still a very inexperienced kisser when things started up with Jackson, but once we started going together, kissing became such a normal part of my day that I didn't even think about it—except that I stopped chewing bubble gum and started chewing mint. Jackson felt me up a lot too. I bought two new bras that clasped in front, so he could open them more easily.

But that's all. It never occurred to me to do anything more. Jackson seemed happy. He never tried to get his hand down my pants or even take my shirt all the way off.

So imagine my feelings. It was Monday morning—

thirteen days after Kim and Jackson got together. I had had the panic attacks, started seeing Doctor Z and become a leper thanks to the Spring Fling debacle and the Xerox horror (don't worry, you'll find out all about *them* soon enough).

I was walking up the steps to school, minding my own business, having done nothing all weekend except watch movies on video with my mother, and Katarina called my name, which she hardly ever does. She was full of news. At her party that weekend[8] she and Heidi had walked into the guest room and found Kim and Jackson on the sofa *with all their clothes off.* Heidi was devastated. Katarina and Ariel were so mad at Kim. Could I believe the nerve? It was so uncool to do that at a party where Heidi was, like she had no feelings at all—and right after Jackson had broken up with me, too.[9]

"They were naked?" I said, almost choking.

"Completely. His thing was out and everything!" Katarina said. "I think I might have even seen it! Of

---

[8] What party? Further proof of my leprosy.

Not only that, she told me about it as if I wouldn't even be remotely hurt at not being invited. Like it was a matter of course that I wouldn't even have known about it! Ag.

She should have broken it to me gently. I had only been a leper for nine days. It's not like I was used to it yet.

[9] What business did Heidi have being devastated about Jackson and Kim? By this point it had been *six months* since their two-month thing. And even if Heidi *was* carrying a torch, which I guess she's entitled to do, why would Katarina bother telling me about it? It only made me feel even worse, if that was humanly possible. There was Heidi, all upset about a boy she went with ages ago, with all these friends supporting her and being angry on her behalf. And here's me, the really injured party, and no one worrying at all.

course," she added, "you don't need my description of *that.*"[10]

"What did they do when you came in?"

"We shut the door again, right away," said Katarina, shrugging. "And like an hour later they came out. Everyone kind of laughed about it, except Heidi was crying in my hot tub and Ariel had to drive her home.[11] Anyway, I thought you'd want to know."[12]

"Thanks," I said.[13]

Katarina hiked her backpack over her shoulder and headed off in the direction of the gym. I stood there, watching her go.

Why did I say thanks, just then? Stuff about Kim and Jackson pressing their naked bodies together was the last thing I wanted to hear.

Naked, naked, naked.

My heart was pounding. I was having trouble breathing. I sat down on the steps and tried to take a deep breath

---

[10] What? She thought I'd seen Jackson's thing, as in penis thing? *And* she thought I'd like to hear that she thinks I've seen it?

I swear, I have no understanding of other human beings. Being a leper suits me perfectly, if my only other choice is being friends with Katarina.

[11] Heidi must have seen it! Otherwise, why would Katarina think *I* had seen it? She must think penis viewing is the norm for Jackson's girlfriends.

[12] So Jackson was getting naked with Heidi and with Kim. But not with me.

[13] Why not with me? Did he not like me as much as those other girls? Was I less attractive than them? Ruby Oliver, not the kind of girl you'd want touching your penis. Ruby Oliver, not exciting enough to try and get her pants off. Ruby Oliver, good enough to kiss, but not good enough to get naked with.

It just kills me.

Not that I wanted to, but why not me?

and think about a peaceful meadow and butterflies flitting about happily.

It didn't help.

I jumped up and ran after Katarina. "Listen, don't tell me that stuff anymore," I said, when I caught up with her.

"What?" she said, looking shocked.

"You're acting like you're being so nice and informative, but you're making other people feel like crap."

"Don't get all upset about it."

"I can't help it," I said. "If you stopped to think for one second, wouldn't you guess that telling me about Kim and Jackson would make me insane? That it would poison my whole day and possibly my entire future life with horrible images of nude bodies and penises that I don't want to think about?"

Katarina sighed. "Don't jump all over me 'cause Jackson broke up with you," she said. "It's not my fault."

"It's your fault I have to think about the two of them naked," I yelled. "Just leave me off your penis information list from now on."

"Fine," she snapped. "You can be sure I will."

She turned and went into the gym.

I felt like an asshole.

But hey: My heart rate was normal, and my lungs felt free and clear.

I took a deep breath.

10. Angelo (but it was just one date.)

Here is why I'm now a leper. I went to the Spring Fling with Jackson, even though he broke up with me before it and was already going out with Kim. So sue me. My ex-boyfriend that I was madly in love with wanted to take me to a dance, and it was only the second formal dance I was going to with a boy, and I had already bought a dress, and who knows? Maybe he'd see me in it and realize he made a big mistake. Really, I think almost any girl in my shoes would have done the same.

Here's the other formal dance I had been to: Homecoming at Garfield High, which is the public school we always drive past on the way to the Chinese restaurant my dad likes the best. I went because my mom's friend Juana (the playwright with the thirteen dogs and four ex-husbands) has a son who goes to Garfield: Angelo.[1] He's a year older than me. I had only met him three or four times before, at Juana's dinner parties. I think he spends a lot of time at his father's house, so he's hardly ever at Juana's when my mom and I go over there.

Angelo seemed all right. He had big brown eyes and curly black hair; sort of a flat, round face. Serene. He dressed kind of hip-hop, which no one does at Tate.

At the dinner parties, we generally got up from the table early and watched TV. He never said too much, probably because Juana is always talk-talk-talking, and also because no one can ever hear at her house anyway, what with all the barking going on.

So Garfield was having a homecoming dance, and I guess Angelo needed a date, which is a little odd because the school has like 1500 students and he's definitely not bad-looking. He didn't even call me and ask directly. Juana called my mother, and my mother asked me if I'd want to go to this thing with Angelo.

I said yes. Not because of Angelo. Because I wanted to go to a dance.

But why was he asking?

Maybe Angelo was such a loser no one at Garfield would go with him. Or maybe he was gay and didn't want to take a girl at all, and Juana thought she was helping him out when really she just had no idea. Or maybe my

---

[1] "But wait!" you careful readers are saying. Weren't you talking about Angelo way back on your first visit to Doctor Z? What does *he* have to do with anything?

mother had told Juana I was unpopular with boys, and so she was making him take me out of pity. Or maybe he was madly in love with some girl Juana didn't like, and I was supposed to distract him?[2]

My mom told me he'd pick me up at eight and not to have so much angst—but I worried for the whole two weeks before the dance. I had used my babysitting money to buy a yellow silk dress from the 1950s, with spaghetti straps—but what if I got all dressed up and he never actually showed? What if he really didn't want to take me, and started being mean, or left me to go off with someone else? What if this was a Stephen King situation?[3]

My mother told me to stop being so insecure. My father asked me sixteen times if I wanted to talk about my feelings of insecurity.

The day of the dance, Angelo arrived on time, wearing a blue suit. He brought me a corsage of yellow roses. My dad took pictures. Juana was driving us, and she acted all hokey, like she was a chauffeur. There were two terriers and a big hairy mutt in the backseat, so we all three sat in the front, squashed in. Juana didn't make us wear the seat belt.

The dance was in the gym, with the lights down low

---

[2] Doctor Z adds the following: "Maybe he liked you and wanted to go to the dance with you, but felt too shy to ask?"

I swear to God I never thought of that.

[3] Stephen King wrote this freaked-out book called *Carrie* about a loser girl who gets asked to the prom by the most popular guy in school, only to find out it's a massive prank when they dump a bucket of pig's blood all over her. It was also a movie.

and decorations everywhere. Angelo and I didn't say much. He got me a cup of fruit punch. A lot of the girls were wearing narrow black gowns and high heels. I felt virginal and young and goofy in my yellow dress with the wide skirt. We danced, and the music was good, and we even slow-danced, which was strange and awkward and nice–holding hands and swaying back and forth.

But the whole thing went on too long. By 8:45, we had danced, stood around, drunk punch, slow-danced, stood around. We had talked to his friends, but the music was too loud to have a real conversation. What else was there to do? We danced some more. Went outside and got some fresh air. I was basically bored from 8:45 until 10:30, when Juana came to pick us up. I sat on his lap on the ride home, since now there was a border collie, a fat Labrador and a mean-looking Doberman in the back.

That was it. I didn't see Angelo again until the next dinner party his mom had. We watched TV, as usual.

Strangely, this anxiety-producing and ultimately boring experience did not lessen my interest in going to another formal dance. I would definitely have gone to the Spring Fling later on in my freshman year, only no one asked me, and I was excited that Jackson was taking me this year. Although I ended up lying to him once again because he never issued a formal invitation. To the *formal*! I mean, aren't you supposed to ask *formally* if you're taking someone to a *formal*? Pete asked Cricket. Bick asked Meghan. Finn asked Kim. Nora asked Jackson's friend Matt. Hello? Are my expectations unreasonable? I don't think so.

But Jackson just assumed we were going. The dance was announced on Friday, three weeks ahead. I figured he'd wait a few days, maybe ask me on Monday, so as not to make a big deal of it. That's what I would have done if I was asking him.[4] So I waited.

And waited.

And waited.

And a week passed, and he hadn't asked me. Cricket and Kim and Nora went shopping for dresses, and I went with them. I tried stuff on, then said I was planning to make the rounds of the vintage stores the next day with my mother.

But I didn't.

Finally, halfway through the second week and five days before we broke up, Jackson and I were talking with Matt and Nora at lunch. "Hey, Roo," Jackson said. "After the Fling would you want to have people over to party on your dock? Because the miniyacht stops nearby."

"Oh, um, sure," I said.

And that's how I knew we were going. I went out and bought a dress, and ended up borrowing $85 from my mother so I could get this great seventies silver wrap thing I found at Zelda's Closet, and to pay it off I was going to have to babysit fourteen hours for this kid who barfs on me nearly every time I go over there.

Then Jackson broke up with me, and after I had been crying and crying alone in my room, I saw the corner of

---

[4] Why *didn't* you ask him?" said Doctor Z.

"Ag." I moaned. "I always know what you're going to say."

"Then we're making progress," she said.

that dress poking out of my closet and it made me cry even harder, because there was nowhere to wear it, and I'd be paying it off for at least a month, and I couldn't believe he let me get excited about the dance and buy a dress, when he was going to dump me.

My parents could hear me sobbing though our paper-thin walls. Mom kept knocking on the door. "Roo, come out here and have dinner with us. I made tofu with diced cauliflower!"

"Elaine," my dad said, "let her have her privacy."

"She's been in there for two hours, Kevin."

"Roo?" asked my dad. "Don't you want to share? Maybe we can help."

"She's not going to talk to us. Get with it. She's a teenager. The best we can hope for is to get some protein into her."

"Sweetie, do you want to talk to just me? Mom doesn't have to come in."

"Kevin!"

"Elaine, you know you make things worse. Maybe you should stay out of this one."

"Ruby," squawked my mom. "If it's a girl thing, you know I'm here for you."

And so on. And so on. I finally put my headphones on to block out the noise.

Tuesday night,[5] my parents took me to a dinner party at Juana's. She lives in this ramshackle house that is so

---

[5] It was on Wednesday that I found out about Kim and Jackson, so at this point I was in the dark.

covered with dog hair you have to wear old jeans when you go, and definitely no black, because you will be insanely furry when you leave. My mom made me go. I wanted to stay home and stare at the phone hoping Jackson would call, but she said I had to socialize.

It was one of the first warm days of spring, and Angelo was out on Juana's front lawn throwing sticks for seven dogs at once. He had this system of three sticks in rotation, so he was throwing constantly. The dogs were going berserk. He was taller than the last time I saw him, and he'd let his hair grow out, so you could see the curls. He was wearing an oversize football jersey and baggy jeans. "Ruby's suffering from a broken heart," my mother announced. "Her boyfriend dumped her. Angelo, you cheer her up. Roo—help him throw the sticks."

"Elaine!" snapped my dad. "When will you learn to give the girl some privacy?"

"People shouldn't have secrets," my mom said. "Besides, he probably already knows. I told Juana everything on the phone."

"Elaine!"

"What?" My mother put her hand on her chest as if to proclaim innocence. "She's my oldest friend!"

"Hey, Roo," said Angelo. "I've got a system going on. Check it out."

"See?" said my mom. "He wants her to help him. Go on, Roo. We'll see you inside."

They went up the steps, my dad muttering at my mother in a low voice.

Angelo and I threw sticks for a while. My hands got

covered with dog slime. We didn't say much, but he did show me how the little mutt named Skipperdee would never drop a stick unless you picked her up and squeezed her. Whenever she brought one back he'd scoop her up with his left hand and squeeze her under his arm while throwing another stick with his right to get the other dogs out of the way; she'd drop the stick, he'd pick it up with his right, put her down with his left, throw the stick and she'd be off again. Also, he had a system of throwing two sticks at the same time, so that the smaller dogs would have a chance against the Labradors, who went for it hardcore.

After a while we went in for dinner. My dad and I ate until our stomachs were sticking way far out, because Juana is a great cook and we'd been eating the macrobiotic-sludge-and-breakfast-cereal diet for weeks.[6] My mother ate a lot, too, bare-faced acting as if fried plantains, spiced shrimp (which I didn't eat), vegetable jambalaya and ice cream with sugared pecans were all part of her normal regime.

"Roo doesn't have a date for the big dance Saturday night," my mother said, as we were all eating dessert on Juana's porch while the dogs roamed around peeing on the grass. "It's on a boat. And she has the most beautiful dress. But no date."

"Mom!" I wanted to die.

---

[6] I thought maybe heartbreak would make me lose my appetite, like it always does to heroines of books, and then I could waste away tragically to nothing and Jackson would see me and I'd be pale and haunted-looking, and he'd realize that he never should have hurt me like that. But no. It turned out my stomach has no idea what's going on in my heart and I could eat just like normal, if only there was normal food in my house to eat.

"Angelo could take her," Juana said, picking up my mother's cue. "He's not doing anything Saturday."

"Mom!" (This, from Angelo.)

"What, honey?" said Juana. "You could take Ruby to her dance. She went with you to homecoming last year. I bet it would be fun."

I looked at Angelo, sure he was thinking what a nightmare it would be to be trapped on a boat with a bunch of prep school kids he didn't even know. "Sure," he said, smiling. "Sounds good."

"Oh. Um. Thanks."

"I should wear a suit, right?"

"Um, yeah."

"Okay. What time?"

"Eight-thirty. The boat leaves at nine."

"No, no, Roo," interrupted my mother. "You two should go to dinner first. It's Roo's treat."

Angelo laughed and gave me a look, like "Ag! Our moms are such freaks." But he said "All right"—and would I like to get Italian, because he'd heard of a good place?

"I'll loan you two the station wagon," said Juana.

"I'll pick you up at seven," said Angelo.

So: I had a date for the Spring Fling, even though I got it in the most embarrassing possible way.

I felt a tiny bit more cheerful all day Wednesday.

Until Kim called Wednesday night with the news about her and Jackson.

From then on, my head felt clogged, like I had a cold, and my chest felt hard and hollow inside. I was in a daze. Literally, everything looked blurry, and my throat was so closed up I could barely talk. Fortunately, Nora and Cricket were still friends with me then, so at lunch both days I got Nora (who had her license) to drive me off-campus for French fries, so I wouldn't have to sit with Kim, or see Jackson in the refectory.

Cricket and Nora basically took the attitude that everything would settle down once I got over the shock. Nora made me some cupcakes and put her arm around me a lot. She framed a photo she had taken of her and me at a lacrosse game. Cricket talked loudly about other subjects and cut cartoons out of the *New Yorker* and put them in my mail cubby. They were happy for Kim, and sorry for me, and they figured I'd be too shattered to deal for a week or two—and then we'd all go back to normal.

But I couldn't even look at Kim, I felt so betrayed. I avoided her even though it meant changing my seat in almost all my classes. More and more every hour, I stopped feeling the sadness I was supposedly going to get over—and started feeling angry. Even though she had been "nice" about the whole thing, and told me herself on the phone, and never kissed him until he had dumped me—I just didn't think she had been nice at all, really. I thought she was a conniving, lying, man-stealing bitch, and I hoped she would fall in a volcano and die a horrible lava death.[7]

But I kept my mouth shut and tried to retain what little dignity I had left.

---

[7] The above paragraph is the product of nearly four months of twice-weekly therapy. Expressing feelings! Yay! Even when saying what you feel makes you sound vindictive and grudge-holding and cranky!

The Friday afternoon before the dance, I came out of lacrosse practice and there was no one to drive me home. Jackson had picked me up every week before, and I was in such a tangle of misery I hadn't even thought to ask anyone in the locker room for a ride. I was the last one to leave, and I went outside and realized I was the only one still there.

I called home from the pay phone. My dad said he'd come pick me up, but it's a forty-minute drive at rush hour, so I sat down on my backpack and tried to do my French homework as the sky grew darker. I wrote about four sentences before I started to cry.

I just sat there, tears going down my cheeks, not even covering my face.

Then Jackson's Dodge pulled up in front of the gym. I felt like an idiot, crying there all by myself–although I have to admit, a tiny part of me thought maybe he'd be deeply moved by how shattered I was and realize I was the girl for him after all. I looked down at my French notebook and tried to get my breathing still. Jackson stopped the car, got out and leaned against the hood.

"Hey, Roo, I was hoping to catch you," he said.

"Yeah?"

"Don't you have a ride? I can take you home, if you want."

"My dad's coming. He's running late."

"How you doing?"

"Pretty good," I lied.

"Can we talk?" He sat down next to me, leaning his back against the red brick of the gymnasium.

"Sure. What about?"

"I'm worried about you. I haven't seen you around all week."[8]

"I'm fine."

"That's not what Nora says."

"Let me speak for myself, okay?"

"And Kim is shattered you won't talk to her."

"Poor baby." My voice was bitter.

"Roo, don't get mean. I'm checking to make sure you're okay. I really care about you."

"Right."

"You do know that, don't you? I hope you're okay with all of this."

---

[8] You know what? At the time, I thought he was being sensitive—but now, it pisses me off. Where does Jackson get off acting all sympathetic and trying to comfort me when he's the entire reason I'm unhappy? What is that about? It actually seems kind of sick. Here's the entry I would have made in *The Boy Book* if only I still had friends to write it with: Breaking Up with Someone: A Few Tips for Boys.

1. If you shatter someone by dumping her, and you're not going to get back together with her ever, don't go following her around to act all concerned about her welfare. Unless you're divorcing and leaving her with three kids. Just leave her alone unless she wants to talk to you. You can't comfort her. You are the bad guy. Just accept it and try not to be such a jerk with your next girlfriend.

2. Don't go wearing the jeans she thinks you look hot in until you're well sure she's over you.

3. Don't tell her she looks pretty.

4. Don't lead her into temptation.

"And if I'm not okay, what are you gonna do about it?" I asked.

"I don't know. We were pretty close. It's hard on me to see you like this."

"Poor you."

"Listen, we can still go to the Spring Fling, if you want. I'd like that, actually. Can we go to the dance?"

"You aren't going with Kim?"

"She has to go out of town with her family. She left this afternoon."

"Won't she be mad?"

"No. She thinks it might cheer you up. She's completely sorry she upset you."

I didn't say anything.

"We'd go as friends," Jackson added.

"I understood that, thank you."

"Aw, don't be sarcastic with me. Let me take you out. You can wear your dress. For old times' sake."[9]

Well, it went on like this for a while longer. The short of it is that I said yes, never even thinking about Angelo, or Kim, or what anyone would say—only thinking about how Jackson still had some feelings for me, would love me again in my silver dress, and how we would stand in the moonlight, looking over the railing at the light playing across the dark water.

---

[9] Just what he said about tennis with Heidi! Plus, our "old times" were only *six days ago* at this point! But I notice these things only in hindsight. At the time, I was oblivious.

11. Shiv (but it was just one kiss.)

You could call Shiv Neel my first official boyfriend. He was
definitely my first voluntary kiss—and the word "girlfriend"
was certainly mentioned by him, in reference to me. But he
was my boyfriend for less than twenty-four hours, so although it was common knowledge all over school that we
were going out, I'm not sure he counts. Anyway, if he *was*
my boyfriend, it's pretty pitiful—because just like Jackson,
he dumped me and I had no idea it was coming.

Is this my pattern for life, to be always dumped with
no warning?[1]

---

[1] Doctor Z: "You're here in therapy to look at your behavior patterns. Recogniz-
ing them is the first step toward changing them, if you desire."
   Me: "But it's not a behavior pattern. It's something other people are doing

Here's what happened. Last year in November, Shiv and I were assigned to do a scene in Drama Elective together. We had to work on it for homework, so we met a few times in an empty classroom during lunch to rehearse. Shiv was (and is) an Indian American boy with a big nose and the most enormous black eyes you've ever seen. I was fascinated by his eyes. He's quite popular–friends with Pete (Cricket's boyfriend, as of Valentine's Day) and this guy Billy Krespin. He plays rugby and basketball, and this year he's going out with Ariel Oliveri. I was glad to do a scene with him. I'd always thought he was cute.

Blah blah blah: All the details of our conversations, and the clever notes about when to schedule rehearsals, and the time we spilled pop all over the teacher's desk, and the time he put his arm around me at assembly (but in the dark so no one could see)–none of that is important. What's important is that one day, he stopped reading his lines, threw his script on the floor, looked into my eyes and said, "Roo, let me ask you something. Will you be my girlfriend?"

"Yes," I said.

He kissed me, then. Really put his arms around me and kissed me. It went through my body like he had

---

to me."

Annoying silence from Doctor Z.

Me: "Seeing that it's a pattern isn't going to help. The No Warning part is about how *there's no warning*. I can't see it coming, so what can I do about it?"

Doctor Z: More silence. Even more annoying, if that's possible.

Me: "Why aren't you talking?"

Her: "I want to let you draw your own conclusions."

flipped some electrical switch and lit me up. His skin was so warm, and he was suddenly so beautiful, and I thought, Oh, *this* is what all the hype is about–because I certainly hadn't felt anything like this with Michael Malone in the woods in my nightgown. We kissed for the rest of lunch period, leaning against the closed classroom door so no one would be able to interrupt us.

Girlfriend! I was somebody's girlfriend! And beautiful, popular, good-kisser Shiv, on top of it all!

Okay, so I'm completely undignified. As soon as school got out, I ran up to Kim, Nora and Cricket on the quad and told them the news. They were completely surprised and excited: Cricket was even jumping up and down. "Shiv! Ag!" she yelled.

"He's *fine,*" said Nora, giggling.

"Have you seen him in his rugby uniform? He has some serious legs," said Kim.

"How did it happen?" Cricket wanted to know.

I told all.

They wanted to know more.

"What did it feel like?"

Electricity.

"What did he smell like?"

Nutmeg.

"What did he taste like?"

I don't know. Person.

"Did he lick your ear?"

No. Gross! (Laughter.)

"Did you grab his butt?"

"Cricket!"

"I would have grabbed his butt."

(More laughter.) "I'm not up to butts," I said. "That's way too advanced."

"Not *down* the pants!" she yelled. "On *top of* the pants."

"Even so. Butt-grabbing on a first kiss is a bit much."

"Oh, I think you can get a nice handful even before the first kiss," said Cricket. (Raucous laughter.)

"You're just going to reach over and squeeze?" I asked.

"Sure, why not?"

"Please. You're all talk."

"No. I would completely do it. On top of the pants, mind you."

And so on.

The next day, I got to school wearing like four times as much lip gloss as usual and Shiv was in the hall, standing next to his mail cubby. "Hey, Shiv," I said to him.

He turned around and walked away.

In Poetry, he didn't look at me.

At lunch in the refectory, he didn't talk to me or sit anywhere near me, but Cricket, Kim and Nora had told all the girls about what happened, so I was pretty busy fielding gossipy questions from Heidi, Ariel, Katarina and the like, so I didn't really have time to think about it much.

In Drama, Shiv and I had to perform our scene.

"What did you think?" I said, after.

"It was okay," said Shiv, his eyes on the ground. Then he grabbed his backpack and left.

After school, I saw him heading for the bus. "Shiv, wait up!" I called.

He kept walking.

By this point, it was obvious he had changed his mind. I felt like an idiot. Had I been a rotten kisser during our session against the door? (This was certainly possible, as I had so little experience.)

Maybe I smelled bad?

Or had there been a booger hanging out of my nose when we stopped kissing?

What could I have done to make him stop liking me?

I thought about it all the time, but I never found out. I felt like a complete loser. I liked him so much, and now he seemed to hate me, and there was no way to turn it around. I was completely helpless.

I never really talked with him again, except to say hi in the halls.

When I told her about Shiv, Doctor Z thought I should ask him what happened. Well, she never says anything quite that directly. What she really said was "Is there a way you could find out?"

"No."

Silence. She was wearing that poncho again.

"Well," I said, after a minute, "I guess I could ask him. But I'd rather die than do that."

More silence. It really is a horrible poncho.

"I don't care, anyway."

Even more silence. Who buys this woman's clothes?

"Well, I guess maybe I kind of do," I went on. "I mean, I do. I liked him, I wanted to kiss him again, we had a good time together. And the whole thing was humiliating. Everyone knowing we were going out, and then with us breaking up so fast after–I felt like people were talking about me."

"Can you ask him?"

I ignored her question. "And this is my life, getting dumped with no warning. Or liking people who don't like me back, or who don't like me *enough,* or not as much as they like someone else. You have the list in front of you: Hutch dumped me for Ariel, Gideon never liked me back, Ben didn't know I was alive, Sky had another girlfriend."

"Story of your life?"

"Exactly. Why is that? I wish I could fix whatever's wrong with me."

"Just one kiss" is never just one kiss. The one with Shiv changed my whole idea about kissing. And when I went to the dance with Jackson, there was "just one kiss"–but it made everything even worse than it was before.

You wouldn't think that was possible, but it was.

After Jackson asked me to the dance, I had a lot of phone calls to make.

First, I had to call up Angelo and tell him not to take me. I was super nervous. I had never called him before, and here I was canceling on him. But he was nice about it. "That's cool," he said. "If he's your boyfriend, you should go with him."

"I don't know if he's my boyfriend," I said.

"Whatever. You should do what you gotta do."

"Okay." There was a weird silence. "There's a party

on the dock by my house after," I said, feeling guilty. "Around eleven. You should swing by if you're around."

"Sure," said Angelo, though I was sure he was only being polite.

"You shouldn't go," said Cricket when I called her. "It's way too complicated."

"It's just as friends," I said.

"Still."

"Kim told him to take me."

"But that's Kim. She feels bad about everything."

"Yeah? She doesn't act like it."

"Trust me," said Cricket. "She does."

"I'm still going," I said. "It'll be fine."

"You shouldn't go," said Nora when she called me.

"I know, but I so want to," I said. "I have that dress."

"You could wear that dress with Angelo," she said.

"I want to go with Jackson. I was always supposed to go with Jackson, he asked me a long time ago."

"Not exactly," she reminded me.

"But still."

"It's your funeral," she said. "Maybe you should come to dinner with me and Matt, to keep it all under control."

Matt added two more onto his reservation, and we all had dinner at the top of the Space Needle, which is this restaurant inside an old World's Fair building that turns around and around so you get a 360-degree view by the time you finish your dinner. They didn't have any vegetarian food, so I ate three side dishes: creamed spinach, mashed potatoes and a salad. Then we drove to the pier in two separate cars, and got on the miniyacht just as it was pulling out.

Here's what I remember from the dance: Cricket looked beautiful, in a pink dress with her sleek blond hair piled on top of her head. Nora looked sexy, showing off her great boobs in a low-cut black thing. She took pictures of us all with her Instamatic.

Jackson touched my hand when we were dancing and told me I was pretty. There was hardly anywhere to sit down. When the band played a slow song, Jackson asked me to dance, and put his cheek against mine as we did. Then he suggested we go upstairs and get some air.

I didn't have a coat. It was freezing on deck. He put his arm around me to keep me warm. It was the first time we were alone all evening. We were standing in the moonlight, looking over the railing at the lake, watching the light play across the dark water, like I'd imagined. Jackson was talking about some anime movie he'd seen.

I wasn't listening.

I was looking at his mouth and feeling his warm hand against my chilly shoulder.

It seemed like the most natural thing in the world to do what I did: I put my hand on his neck and kissed him.

He kissed me back.

I thought: This is right. I forgive everything. He wants me again. We'll be together.

Then he pushed me away. "Ruby," Jackson said in a

strange, loud, public voice. "What are you doing? That's not how it is, now. We're here as friends. You know I'm with Kim."

I looked across the deck. Standing there, looking at us—Heidi Sussman and Finn Murphy. Jackson pushed past them and ran down a set of steps.

●

As soon as I was alone on the deck of the boat, I had a panic attack. Heidi and Finn had disappeared, and there was no one out there except Meghan and some seniors, down at the other end, plus one couple who had their tongues down each other's throats. I felt so dizzy I had to hold on to the railing to stand up, my heart was hammering, my breath was coming in tiny gasps; I felt like there was no oxygen, and I broke out in a sweat, even though it was freezing. Eventually I staggered over to a bench.

Noel came out and sat next to me. He's the boy from Painting Elective who sent me that carnation with the goofy rhyme on Valentine's Day. "How do I love thee? As high as pigs can fly." He was wearing a tuxedo, which no other boys were doing (they wore suits), and he lit a cigarette with an old-fashioned silver lighter.

This Noel is one of those not-quite-friends-with-everybody people who never seems like he's being serious. He's very ironic about Tate and everything it stands for (preppy white lacrosse players driving BMWs), but he's got a lot of confidence and no one gives him any crap. His shaggy blond hair sticks out in a ridiculous way that I think probably requires hair gel. His left eyebrow is pierced. That night, his combat boots were sticking out under his tux, big steel toes glinting in the moonlight.

If Noel has girlfriends, he has them out of school. He came to the dance alone, which almost no one could get away with, but Noel is such a man of ironic distance that he pulled it off and no one thought he was a leper.

"Hey, Ruby," he said, sinking down next to me on the bench near the ship's railing. "I hear there's a party at your house, and now your boyfriend's in a twist over something and you don't even have a ride to your own fête. Can that be true, or is it a load of Tate gossip?"

I couldn't believe I'd let Jackson tell people that party was still on. He'd probably invited half the junior and sophomore classes. "How do you know I don't have a ride?" I asked. (Would Jackson really leave without me?)

"Are you kidding?" Noel scrunched up his nose and took a drag off his cigarette. "It's all over the boat."

"Ag. Well, then I'm sure no one's coming to my house."

"You better believe they are. Five people asked me if I was going. Ariel Oliveri. Katarina Dolgen. It's going to be a scene."

"Oh, no."

"If I'm invited, I'll give you a ride home."

"Of course you're invited. I–I haven't had the best week. Jackson told everybody about it. It was his idea."

Noel smiled. "That's okay. I know. I keep up on my Ruby Oliver news."

I was so grateful, I felt like Noel was a knight in shining armor. He gave me his jacket to wear and hustled me into his car. We drove back to my house and my parents had set out coolers full of soft drinks down on the end of the dock where the boats are–plus a bunch of folding chairs and some candles in paper bags, which looked so pretty. People were already standing around when I arrived: Matt and Nora (who said she was tired and had her mom pick her up right after I got there)[2]; Ariel and Shiv; Katarina and Kyle; a bunch of junior friends of Jackson's; Shep "Cabbie" Cabot and a senior girl with big boobs; some sophomores I knew from lacrosse. Finn and Heidi came a little while later. Cricket[3] and Pete never showed.

It was a beautiful night, I was the hostess of a party full of popular people wearing gorgeous clothes; there was a boy in a tux by my side. It should have been great.

Instead, I was shattered.

Someone handed me a beer. I don't remember who. I'd never really had more than a couple of sips before that, or maybe a little wine at one of my mom's opening night parties–but I drank the whole can. And I'd like to blame what happened next on that–only I can't, because as Doctor Z says, I am in charge of myself.

Here's a list of semi-beer-induced bad things that happened at the dock party, and I admit that three of them are my own stupid fault:

One: I held hands with Noel. I grabbed it on purpose when Finn and Heidi arrived. I felt like I wanted protection. He kept holding it for a while, and I liked it. But

---

[2] Because she was mad at me on Kim's account and was basically never going to talk to me again.

[3] Ditto.

I felt weird about it the next day. I hadn't meant to be flirtatious.[4]

Two: It soon became clear that the story Heidi was spreading around about what she saw on the boat did *not* involve Jackson kissing me back—which he did for at least twenty seconds, I swear. Heidi's story[5] involved Jackson being a faithful saint who was only doing a favor taking a poor, rejected four-eyed ex to a dance when she had no other date, but then she (me) made this huge unwanted pass at him and he had to push her (me) away, in order to remain true to the no-butt bitch he was currently dating (Kim), which of course he would, because even though he couldn't really care about her (Kim), he was still such an excellent guy.[6]

---

[4] All right. Maybe I had. In fact, I certainly had. He was cute. I wanted some attention. I wanted to feel like less of a loser. This admission, courtesy of yet another therapy session with Doctor Z.

[5] Which I found out by blatantly listening in on a conversation she and Ariel were having.

[6] In H&P, Mr. Wallace is always talking about how the media "spins" the facts one way or another, depending on political agendas. Like a Democratic newspaper would emphasize how much the former President Clinton did for the economy, while a Republican paper might focus on how he never seemed to keep it in his pants. Heidi put her own spin on the Jackson/Roo drama, probably because she still likes Jackson. No one ever asked me for my spin, except for Doctor Z—but here it is, anyhow:

Jackson *was* cheating on Kim when he asked Roo to the dance, because Jackson still likes Roo; they went out for six months, after all. He slow-danced with Roo and made her feel all sexy. He took her out for a moonlit walk on the deck of the boat. He put his arm around her, not like friends at all. He was being romantic, dammit! And he kissed her back when she kissed him, because the whole kissing thing was what he'd wanted all along.

Then he changed his tune when he got caught.

Three: Angelo Martinez showed up! I never in a zillion years thought he would, even though I invited him. But there I was, talking to Noel and feeling dizzy from the beer and also annoyed that all these people were more than happy to drink my parents' pop and stand on our dock while slavering over my multiple rejections and humiliations. I was trying to explain to Noel how I didn't ever want to talk about Jackson again and did he think Jackson still liked me? when I glanced over at Katarina and who was she talking to but Angelo! He was wearing chinos and a sweatshirt–and he was *holding a corsage.*

"Hi," I said, walking over.

"Hi," he said.

"Is this your new boyfriend, Roo?" asked Katarina.

Angelo ignored her, and handed me the corsage in its clear plastic box. Yellow roses, like at Homecoming. "I paid for it in advance," he said, "before you called. So I figured, why not pick it up and bring it over?"

"Thanks."

"I hope your boyfriend won't mind." Angelo opened the box for me and lifted out the flowers. I looked down at the pink carnations from Jackson, sagging but still pinned to the strap of my dress.

I ripped them off and stamped them into the ground with the heel of my silver shoe. "He won't mind," I said, "I can promise you that." I stood on tiptoe and kissed Angelo on the cheek. "These flowers are just what I needed tonight," I said. "Thanks a lot."

"No problem," he said, and then he bent down and

kissed *my* cheek, only a little closer to the mouth than a normal cheek kiss. A jolt went down my spine.

"Roo, what the hell?"

I turned, and there was Jackson, striding down the length of the dock with his tie loosened. The smashed carnations. The kiss. He had seen it all.

"What are you doing here?" I asked, stepping back from Angelo.

"Who's this guy?"

"We weren't–"

"I can't believe you!"

"Me?"

"I was coming back to talk," Jackson said under his breath, his lips close to my ear. "I've been driving all over, thinking about things. I came back, because I felt bad about what happened on the boat." He was sweating. I had no idea what to say. "I thought you cared about me," Jackson went on. "But obviously none of it ever meant anything."

"What?"

"I can't believe you're here, making out with some guy."

"Jackson!"

He turned around and stomped back to his car.

When I turned around, Angelo was gone too.

Four: My mom found a beer can. "Roo, how did this get here? I'm so disappointed in you; don't you know some of your friends are driving? blah blah blah." Not even important in the grand scheme of things, except that

I had to listen to an endless lecture when I was frankly in no condition to deal.

So there I was, my mom yelling at me, Heidi talking crap about me, weirded out by the Noel dynamic, Angelo probably mad at me, Jackson thinking I was cheating on him/getting over him too quickly/generally skanky—and you'd think things couldn't get worse, but ha! It's my life. Things can always get worse.

Five: I was standing in front of our house getting lectured by Elaine Oliver, who gives loud and obnoxious monologues *for a living* and was therefore on a tremendous and highly dramatic rant, when Meghan came walking down the dock. The other kids were still partying like thirty yards away, down where the boats were. I had seen Meghan briefly at the dance, and she looked stunning in a black strapless dress and a string of pearls around her neck. Very different from her usual scruffy prepster look. "Hi, Mrs. Oliver," she said, polite as can be.

"Meghan, how nice to see you!" My mom suddenly turned on the charm. "Did you have fun at the Spring Fling?"

"Yes," she said. "I dropped Bick off and I'm just getting back. I saw the candles. Roo, are you having a party?"

"Sure," said my mother, all hostessy. You would never believe this was the same woman who only seconds before was screaming that I was an "inconsiderate recklessly endangering illegal party monster" about beer *that I didn't even buy.* "Would you like a pop?" Mom said to Meghan. "Your dress is beautiful, sweetie."

"Thanks."

My mom walked over to one of the coolers to get a drink.

"Roo, how come you didn't invite me?" Meghan asked, as soon as my mother was out of earshot.

"What?"

"To your party." Her voice was hurt. "Did you think I wouldn't know about it? I live practically next door."

To tell the truth, I simply hadn't thought of it. Sure, Meghan drove me to school every day. Sure, we'd talk about stuff and get drive-thru Starbucks, and borrow money off each other, and sing along to the radio–but I never thought of her as my friend. I guess I figured she'd be off at some party with Bick and the Whipper and a bunch of seniors, and she wouldn't care what my crew of sophomores and juniors were up to.

"I–I meant to," I stammered. "It was an accident. Jackson did everything. I didn't have much to do with it."

"Are you mad at me about something?" Meghan asked. "I thought we were friends."

"I forgot to invite Noel, too," I said. "He wasn't mad. He just came along. Please don't take it personally."

"I'd never have a party and not invite you," Meghan said. "We go to school together every single day. We're neighbors." She was shivering, her skinny arms looking cold and raw against her black silk dress.

"Here's your pop, Meghan," my mother said, coming back with an icy can. "I hope ginger ale is okay; it's all we had left. I looked for a Coke, but I couldn't find one, so you're stuck with the unpopular drink."

"Perfect," said Meghan, smiling sweetly at my mom. "I'm an unpopular girl. Do you mind if I take it with me? I'm completely tired. I should be getting home."

I went inside to the bathroom and had another panic attack.

●

Monday after the dance, no one would talk to me. Meghan didn't show up to drive me to school, so my mom eventually took me. Kim was back from her family's weekend trip, and I could feel her and Jackson ignoring me from miles away.

I tried to talk to Cricket and Nora, but Cricket just said, "Later, okay, Roo? We've got stuff to do," and the two of them went off toward the refectory and then avoided me the rest of the day. Katarina and her set were pleasant enough, but I could tell they wanted to know what was going on with Angelo and Jackson so they could spread it around, so I tried not to get into conversations with them.

The only person who was nice to me was Noel. We had Painting Elective together, and he walked with me across the quad afterward, barefaced lighting up a cigarette with his paint-covered hands, even though any teacher could have seen him at any time.

"Thanks for the ride Saturday," I said.

"At your service."

"I don't know what I'd have done without you."

"Someone else would have given you a lift."

"Maybe."

"You were having a party, Roo."

"I guess."

"You're like the warrior princess of the Tate universe," said Noel. He lowered his voice to sound like a TV announcer: "No matter what they said about her. No matter what people thought! Ruby Oliver was undaunted. She gave parties, she kissed other people's boyfriends, she held hands with strange men. In her magical silver dress, she kicked the asses of one and all who dared to stand in her way. . . ."

I laughed. "Then why do I feel like a leper?"

"The warrior princess was covered with the strange green spots of leprosy," Noel went on in his announcer voice, "but that did not diminish her charms nor impair her miraculous kung fu and painting abilities."

I kickboxed the air in front of me. "Tcha!"

"Seriously," said Noel. "You're not afraid to be seen with me? After what people are saying?"

"What do you mean?"

"At least three people have asked me if we're going out now."

"You're kidding."

"Cricket asked what I thought of the Dalí poster in your bedroom."[7]

"She did?"

"And Nora asked if we were an item."

"Nora? Why wouldn't she ask *me*?"

---

[7] It's a painting by this surrealist artist named Salvador Dalí who had the most amazingly strange mustache. It's called *Soft Watch at Moment of First Explosion* and it shows this almost gloopy-looking pocket watch, really huge, which is self-destructing. I love it.

"And Josh asked if I was 'doing you' behind Jackson's back all along."

"Josh is a moron."

"Yeah, but he's asking what people want to know." He sucked on the butt of his cigarette and then stubbed it out on the bottom of his combat boot. I wondered if Noel had seen me sort of kissing Angelo, and guessed he probably hadn't. But he would hear about it soon enough, that was for sure.

I stared at Noel. He was delicate, underweight, wearing a leather coat.

He looked me in the eye. "I don't mind if they're saying that stuff," he said. "It doesn't bother me."

I wondered if he had held my hand because he liked me—or because he was being nice. I wondered if he liked girls at all. It was hard to tell with Noel, the way it was hard to tell when he was serious or when he was joking. Like he was on the cross-country team, but he never seemed to care about winning or not winning, the way Jackson did. And he smoked cigarettes, but was otherwise a straight-edge; no beer, no drugs, no meat, no toxins. He even drank carrot juice.

He was a disorienting person.

"I'll tell them whatever you want me to," he went on. "Nothing ever happened. Or we've been together since Christmas. Or I fondled your digits against your will. Or we had an incredible one-night stand. Whatever you want me to say. I don't give a crap what Cricket and Nora think. Or Jackson Clarke, even if he is bigger than me. They're a bunch of Tate idiots, anyway."

"Those people are my friends, Noel," I said, suddenly feeling defensive.

"Some friends."

"What does *that* mean?"

"I mean, if those are your friends you've got no need for enemies."

"There's just a misunderstanding. It'll all blow over."

Noel shook his head. "You think better of this scene than I do, Ruby. Don't you see how fake those girls are? Let it go. Have a laugh about it when you're older. Forget that junk."

I wanted to believe him, to skip off to some punk-rock hangout and develop ironic distance and start over in a universe where it didn't matter what any of these people thought about me. But I couldn't.

I just loved them.

"Trust me," he said. "You don't need Jackson Clarke or Cricket McCall to have a life."

I'm not ironic. I'm—whatever the opposite of ironic is. Oversensitive. Overly sincere.

"Why are you following me around, Noel?" I said. "Fuck off."

Not surprisingly, I had another panic attack shortly after this Noel situation, and on Tuesday I pretended I was sick and stayed home all day, eating jelly candies and reading a mystery novel. Actually, since I didn't know what a panic attack was yet, I figured I was probably dying of some heart attack/lung disorder horror, but I told my mom

I had a bad headache and cramps. She let me stay home, and then fussed over me for the first two hours, bringing me muscle-relaxant teas and hot water bottles while popping back and forth to the desk in the living room where she was doing her freelance copyediting. Finally, finally, she had to go out to a meeting and I was able to take a shower, have a good cry and eat the pound of spearmint jelly candies I knew my dad had hidden in his office.

Wednesday I went to school and flunked a math test I'd forgotten about. Kim called me a slut under her breath in H&P, and Mr. Wallace heard her and gave a lecture on the negative effects of labels, and how words like that serve to limit women's sexual expression, and how there's a whole history of words that basically mean *slut* [8] and yet there are no equivalent epithets for men whatsoever, and didn't *that* say something about how women are viewed in our culture? He said a more accurate term could be: "a girl who's using sexuality in an attempt to gain approval from the opposite sex. . . ." Or, if you look at it a different way, "a liberated, open girl who likes boys and feels comfortable expressing affection, but is misunderstood." Blah blah blah.

I'm sure he meant well, but I wanted to call Kim a megaslut right back and not think about it anymore.

I let three easy shots in when we played Nightingale Girls' School (I play goalie), and the whole lacrosse team was annoyed with me. And then after the game, I agreed

---

[8] Trollop! Hussy! Tart! Chippie!

to go to the movies with Cabbie, this rugby player I barely know who randomly showed up to watch girls' lacrosse— and who probably only asked me out because he's heard I'm a slut, thanks to Mr. Wallace's epic discussion of that word, its historical context and its linguistic precursors, which had been the sole topic in the refectory and on the quad for the rest of the school day.

I don't know why I said yes. I didn't want to go out with him, really.

But I didn't want to stay home on Friday night, either.

I thought I was putting on a pretty good face at dinner that night with my parents. Just sitting there, pushing my brown rice around the plate like usual. But then I had the fifth panic attack, right there at the dinner table, and that was when my mom decided I was surely becoming anorexic, my father was certain I was suicidal and my mother made Meghan's mom come over and then called Juana and then called Doctor Z.[9]

I started therapy the next day, finished writing the first draft of the Boyfriend List Friday morning—and then threw it in the trash at school like the mental patient that I am.

Monday morning, I got to school late because I took the bus (Meghan hadn't shown up since the Spring Fling party) and found a Xerox in my mail cubby. It was a grayed-out copy of the pretty, cream-colored stationery

---

[9] Which, now that I think of it, means that Angelo almost certainly knows I'm a severe neurotic with anxiety problems, since my mom told Juana and Juana probably told him.

Not that he'd ever speak to me again, anyway, after what happened.

my grandmother bought me, with Ruby Denise Oliver across the top. The paper had been crumpled and then pressed flat again on the glass of a photocopier.

It was my first draft of the boyfriend list for Doctor Z, out of order, with arrows drawn all over, names crossed out, names squeezed in, some silly doodles.

I looked at the wall of mail cubbies. The same Xerox was still sticking out of about ten mailboxes in the sophomore section, and a few more in the junior and senior sections—but it was clear that most people had already picked up their mail. I grabbed the few that were left and stuffed them in my backpack. And then yet again, my heart started hammering and I felt like I couldn't breathe. Was I going to die of a heart attack out of sheer humiliation? I stumbled over to the girls' bathroom and sat down on the floor, wheezing and staring at the list. Horror.

Who had done this? Why?

Finn. Hutch. Gideon. Chase. Shiv. Jackson. Noel. Cabbie. All of them were Tate boys, though Chase and Gideon were long gone. Then Adam. Ben. Tommy. Sky. Michael. Angelo. Billy. No one would know who they were.

Except there *was* an Adam Bishop who took Painting Elective. And Ben Ambromowitz was a sophomore I knew from swimming. And Tommy Parrish had gone out with Cricket in ninth grade. Sky Whipple (the Whipper) was captain of the crew team. Michael Sherwood was in my Geometry class. Chase Hilgendorf was a cute freshman lots of girls had their eyes on. And Billy Alexander was a senior friend of Bick's—or there was Billy Krespin, my Bio/Sex Ed lab partner.

Except for Angelo and Gideon, every single one of these names looked like the name of a boy who currently went to Tate.

What would people think?

That it was a list of boys I planned to sink my slutty claws into.

That it was a list of boys I already *had* sunk my slutty claws into.

That by putting the boys in order, I was somehow rating them. How good-looking they were; how good they were at kissing; how good they were in bed.

Whatever the interpretation, the list made it seem like I was basically a man-eater, chewing my way through Tate's hunky population without so much as a batted eye for the poor, vulnerable girlfriends whose hearts were breaking right and left.

Anyone could have pulled the list out of the trash on Friday, but Kim was the only person who would have Xeroxed it.

I skipped first period and pretty much hid in the bathroom. Then I forced myself to go to class—Drama Elective. I could see the Xerox sticking out of some people's binders as we stumbled through a reading of Ibsen's *A Doll's House,* sitting in a circle and changing parts whenever the drama teacher noticed people getting too restless. Later, in the hallways, I could hear whispers as I went by.

Tommy Parrish and Ben Ambromowitz gave me weird looks.

The Whipper pinched my butt in the hallway.

Cabbie and Billy Alexander talked crap about me where I could easily overhear.

Ariel, because she's dating Shiv, slammed into me so hard in the refectory line that my shoulder got bruised. "Ooh," she said loudly, "I guess I wasn't thinking about other people's feelings."

Michael from Geometry leered and waggled his eyebrows, then passed me a note that said, "You're on my list too."

Chase Hilgendorf said hi to me in the hall, then cracked up laughing.

In class, Finn growled at me under his breath: "You've made everything worse, you know."

"What?" I asked.

"Why would you go and do that?" he whispered. "You know what Kim's like when she's mad."

"I didn't write it for everyone to see," I started to say–but he turned away from me and wouldn't talk anymore.

It went on like this all week. I went from being just a leper to being a leper *and* a famous slut.[10] By Friday, the girls' bathroom in the main building had a ton of anti-Roo graffiti.

---

[10] The only person who said anything even semidirectly to me was Nora, when I asked her if she was mad at me about the Xerox, and she said "Give me some credit, already," as if she didn't believe whatever was being said about it. But she was furious about my kissing Jackson when he belonged to Kim and breaking the Rules for Dating in a Small School—so it wasn't like she was lending me any support.

"Who does Ruby Oliver think she is?" (This in Kim's writing.)

"Mata Hari."

"Pamela Anderson."

"God's gift to the male sex."

"Ruby Oliver is a ____ (fill in the blank)."

"Lousy friend."

"Fantasist."

"Slut." (Kim again.)

"Ho. Remember? We can't say *slut* anymore."

"Trollop." (Kim.)

"Hussy."

"Tart."

"Chippie."

"What is that boyfriend list? Your interpretation here."

"Guys she's blown, in order of size."

"I hear she goes on her knees behind the gymnasium."

"Guys she's done, in order of conquest."

"Guys she's done behind other girls' backs." (Kim.)

"Do you think she really did Noel DuBoise? Who has he gone out with, anyway?"

"Do you think she really did Hutch? Gross."

"Maybe he's an acquired taste."

And in Nora's round printing: "Come on, ladies. She may be a lousy friend, but doesn't *everyone* make lists of boys they think are cute? That's probably all it is."

"I hope she's using birth control."

"I heard she might have an STD."

"Do you think she gave it to Billy A? He's so hot."

"Billy Alexander keeps condoms in his back pocket."

"So does Cabbie."

"Big deal if she did Cabbie. Hasn't everybody done him by now?"

"It's still skanky."

I tried to wash it all off with a wet paper towel, but you could still read it with no trouble, especially the parts in black Magic Marker. I borrowed a scrub brush and some spray cleaner from the janitor's closet and was down on my knees trying to get it off when Kim came in.

It was the first time I'd seen her alone since she started going out with Jackson. She ignored me and started putting her hair up with a barrette.

"You made that Xerox, didn't you?" I said.

"What if I did? People should know what kind of person you are."

"And did you start all this on the wall?"

"No." She kept fixing her hair.

"You didn't?"

"That's none of your business."

"I know your writing, Kim."

"So why are you asking me, then?"

"It was a list I had to make for my shrink, okay? I have to see a therapist now, and she made me write a list." Kim was quiet. "I'm all screwed up."

"Tell me about it." Her voice was sarcastic.

"I'm losing my mind," I said. "Because my best friend stole my boyfriend. I trusted her and she stabbed me in the back."

"I didn't steal him. It was fate."

"How is that different from stealing? Enlighten me."

"We're in love," she said hotly.

"You were supposed to be my friend."

"I told you, we never meant for it to happen. It's one of those things that's meant to be."

"Then what was he doing with me at the Spring Fling?"

"He was trying to be nice, Roo. He told me all about it."

"That's what *he* says."

"I trust him," said Kim. "I know exactly what went on. It's you I can't trust."

"Me?" The wet scrub brush had dropped into my lap and was soaking water into my cords, but I didn't care. "What did I ever do to make you not trust me?"

"I could never trust you with Finn," she spat out. "You were always flirting with him."

"I never even talked to him," I said.

"No, you gave him looks, and batted those eyelashes, and crossed those legs of yours in your fishnets, and avoided him, like if you talked to him for one minute he was sure to fall madly in love with you."

"What?"

"I saw you at the Halloween party. What you two were like when you were alone together."

"We were never alone!"

"Well, it sure looked like something. He went on and on about how funny you were, after. How he was a jaguar/Freddy Krueger or something."

"Freddy Krueger kitty cat."

"Whatever. Like an in-joke."

"He was a panther, anyway."

"That's not the point. You were all over him."

"I was not."

"Ever since then. Or even before that. You two move around each other like there's some big secret between you that no one else knows about. He was always asking about you."

"Kim! Nothing happened."

"It doesn't matter," she snapped. "I don't want him anymore anyway. But you should think about what kind of friend you are before you go around saying I stole your boyfriend." She zipped her backpack shut with a sudden noise. "Take a look at yourself, Ruby," she said, heading for the door. "I may be a bitch, making that Xerox, but if it makes you think at all about how you act, how you cross lines and kiss people you shouldn't kiss, and flirt around all over the place without considering how other people feel—then I'm glad I did it."

And she was gone.

My dad always wants me to empathize with other people. Consider their positions, work on forgiveness. And now that this whole debacle is nearly four months behind me, I do think Kim was right about me and Finn. Not that he has a thing for me, not that I have a thing for him, not that we did anything wrong, exactly—but I did stay out of his way because I somehow thought I was capable of stealing Kim's boyfriend, like there was something underground there; and he did give me looks, especially when I wore fishnets, and I did like it. The whole dynamic between us was not what it should be if he was dating my best friend. I mean, I put him on the list—even though nothing even remotely romantic ever happened between us. That *must* mean something.

So I was wrong. About that. And I stopped wearing the fishnets.

Kim believes in fate; she believes Tommy Hazard is out there somewhere waiting to be her one and only; and now she believes Jackson is it. Him. Her Tommy Hazard. She believes he didn't kiss me back, or come back to the Spring Fling party with the idea of getting back together with me—because she wants him to be the perfect guy she's always been looking for. I couldn't have been that cranked about Jackson if I was flirting with Finn, she thinks—and she was half angry with me about the Finn thing anyway, which made it all the easier to justify starting up with Jackson.

Kim plays by the rules. She spends all this time being a good person, doing charity stuff, getting good grades and being the nice overachiever the Doctors Yamamoto want her to be. When someone (me) doesn't live up to her standards, she dishes out what she thinks they deserve. And she thought I deserved the Xerox.

If I'd ever told my mother about what happened with the boyfriend list (which I never did), she would have said that Kim is a double-crossing backbiter. Then she'd have said I should vent my rage, forget all about Kim, get on with it and go eat some soy-based product.

My dad tells me to forgive.

My mom tells me to forget.

But I don't want to do either. Just because I understand where Kim was coming from doesn't mean that I think what she did was right.

And I can't forget her. We go to school together.

●

The Monday morning after my confrontation with Kim in the girls' bathroom, I was waiting at the bus stop near my house, reading the comics page of the *Times* and drinking juice from a carton—when Meghan's Jeep pulled up to the curb. "Your mom said I'd find you here," she said, leaning over to yell out the passenger window. "Get in."

I got in. She stepped on the gas.

We drove in silence for about ten minutes, until she pulled into the Starbucks drive-thru and ordered our usual vanilla cappuccinos. "My treat."

"How come?"

Meghan looked at me. "You had a bad week."

"Yeah. I'm having a bad life."

"And you paid me gas money in advance," she said. "So now I owe you, since I didn't drive you."

Meghan turned on the radio and we sang stupid songs together at the top of our lungs until we got to school.

12. Billy (but he didn't call.)

Four weeks and 8.5 therapy sessions after the Xerox went around school.

"Billy was this boy who said he'd call me last summer but he didn't call," I told Doctor Z. "I kissed him at a party in July. Everyone was wearing togas. You know, made from sheets. His had daisies and ducklings all over it. I think he goes to Sullivan."

"You kissed him? Or he kissed you?" she wanted to know.

"He kissed me. We were waiting in line for the bath-room. It was a dark hallway."

"Then what?"

"He squeezed my boob through like eight layers of

folded blue sheet. It was my first boob squeeze, but I'm not sure it should count."

"Because of the sheets?"

"Yeah. Anyway, I gave him my number, and he never called. I waited by the phone like an idiot, too."

"Uh-huh."

"Now, what I want to know is, why do you ask a girl for her number and then not call? To me, the hard part would be asking for the number, or leaning in to kiss someone you've hardly met when you're wearing a sheet covered in little yellow duckies. After you've done those things, you know she'll go out with you if you call. So why not call?"

Doctor Z didn't say anything. She doesn't say anything a lot of the time.

"Unless you suddenly find her disgusting or stupid or something," I went on, "and only ask for her number because you already kissed her, so you think you *have* to. But actually, Billy didn't have to. I would have been perfectly happy to have a toga-party kissing escapade and leave it at that! It was only once he said he'd call that I wanted him to call, and then there I was, running home to check my messages, and there weren't any.[1] It was all so dumb."

"How long did this go on for?"

"Two weeks. After two weeks I figured he was never calling."

"Ruby," said Doctor Z. "I'm going to say something to

189

---

[1] I swear, I am the only person at Tate who doesn't have a cell phone. Even the fifth graders have them.

you, and if you feel it's not accurate, say so and we'll move on. But it is time to be frank. From my observation, you have a lot of passive patterns in place right now that aren't making you happy."

Translation from therapy-speak: I sit around too much, waiting for people to do stuff and angsting about stuff they've done, without doing anything myself. I could have gotten Billy's number at the party, could have called him, could have made it happen, if I'd wanted it. I could have made up with Meghan just by calling her and apologizing, but I sat there at the bus stop every morning, letting her be angry, until she felt sorry for me and gave me a ride. I could have called Cricket and Nora. I could have told Jackson the truth more, could have insisted we watch something other than boring anime movies. Slept in instead of watching cross-country meets on Saturday mornings. Refused to hang around with Matt all the time. Could have not answered the phone, if Jackson called at five p.m. when he said he'd call in the morning. Could have asked him to the dance. Could have taken off his damn pants myself, if I wanted them off. "Go on," I said to Doctor Z.

"I want to ask, do you see any common pattern between your behavior and your mother's?"

What? My mother was the least passive person I knew. *"Elaine Oliver! Feel the Noise!* Express your rage!" I shouted. "Are you kidding?"

"Both of you are excellent talkers, that is certainly true," said Doctor Z.

I had never thought of myself as being like my mom that way. Did Doctor Z really think I was an excellent talker? *Was* I an excellent talker? Hmmm. Ruby Oliver, excellent talker. "Why do you think she's passive?" I asked.

"You tell me."

Ag. How come these shrinks won't give you the answers when they know them already? "Um," I said, excellent talking ability rapidly deteriorating.

Silence.

I thought as hard as I could. Nothing.

"Didn't you tell me a story about a taco suit?" Doctor Z prompted.

"Yeah."

"And a macrobiotic diet?"

"Uh-huh."

We sat there for another minute.

"Do you think there's any kind of power struggle going on in your home?" she finally asked.

"Maybe. Yeah."

"What's the dynamic that you see?"

I had a rush of memories. My mom: shredding tissues and sitting by the phone the time my dad went on a business trip and didn't call. My mom: spending a weekend at a plant show, bored out of her mind. My mom: going to that Halloween party in the same dumb silly hat as last year after wasting her entire day on the taco. My mom: cleaning the house while my dad ran a 10K with some friends, then having a two-hour fight with him over interpretations of the mayor's education policy, which she doesn't actually care about *that* much. My mom: going macrobiotic after my father made plans to spend every weekend greenhousing the southern deck, when she wanted to go on day hikes and take a family vacation. My mom: not on tour right now with her latest one-woman show, because Dad couldn't go with her.

My mom, always "expressing her rage," but never really getting her way.

She does a thousand tiny things she hopes he'll appreciate—clipping articles from the paper, putting a vase of flowers on his desk, leaving notes whenever she goes out—but he doesn't fully see them, unless she points them out. And she never stops doing them, and never stops being angry that he doesn't appreciate her enough.

The all-about-your-mom analysis was true—but also very annoying. I kind of hate it when Doctor Z is right, especially when it makes me a cliché: Ruby Oliver, repeating her mother's patterns. Still, I decided to ask Shiv Neel what happened last year. I couldn't stop thinking about it, once I had told the story in therapy: how we'd flirted for weeks during our Drama rehearsals, how he put his warm arm around me in assembly, how we kissed in the empty classroom, how beautiful his eyes were, how good it felt to be his girlfriend, even if it was only for an afternoon.

And then—how he disappeared on me.

Shiv is popular. I knew I'd never get him alone in the refectory or on the quad. He's always surrounded by the adoring Ariel or a bunch of loud rugby players. But he's also on the Sophomore Committee, which is Tate's round-table way of having a class president/vice president/treasurer, etc.–and that meant he stayed late on Wednesdays.

I skipped lacrosse practice and waited after school until his meeting was over, reading a book outside the classroom door. My hands were soaked with sweat, I was so nervous, but I took deep breaths and didn't have a panic attack. He came out. I stood. "Hey, Shiv, do you have a minute?"

"I guess," he said. "What's up?"

"Well, you probably know Jackson dumped me."

"Uh-huh."

"And, um, I–can we go somewhere?" Two brainy-looking committee members were standing right next to us in the hall.

"Okay." Shiv shrugged as if he didn't care what we did.

"I don't mean *go somewhere* go somewhere," I said, remembering that he surely thought I was a slut, and after all, last time the two of us had been alone we'd been all over each other. "I mean, outside on the steps."

"I got it." He looked at me like I was an idiot. We went outside and sat down.

I looked at my shoes. They were scuffed.

I fiddled with my fingernails, and chewed on one of them a bit.

I got out my pencil, and tapped it on my knee.

"Roo," said Shiv. "I don't have all day."

"Okay. Do you remember you once asked me to be your girlfriend?"

"It wasn't that long ago."

"But then, somehow, it never happened?"

"Uh-huh."

"I, well—I wondered why you changed your mind. I'm not mad or anything. Only, I'm trying to figure stuff out, since the Jackson thing, and I know it wasn't a big deal, and maybe you don't want to explain, but I've been thinking about it, I guess, and . . ." Blah blah blah. I went on for some ridiculous amount of time, sounding completely lame and saying "like" just about every other word.

Eventually, finally, I got it all said and shut up so he could answer.

"Roo, you were laughing at me," Shiv said, looking down at his own shoes now. "I heard you on the quad."

"What?"

"I heard you, with Cricket and Kim and those guys, cracking up over what a jerk you thought I was."

"That's not true!"

"I was there."

"I didn't."

"You yelled 'Gross!' " he said. "I know I'm not wrong. And you were laughing all over the place, like I was some big joke."

"Ag!" I said. "That's not how it happened."

"And something about I smelled like nutmeg? Like you were disgusted by kissing an Indian or something." His voice was bitter. "I wasn't going to go out with you after that. I didn't even want to look at you for months."

"Nutmeg is good, Shiv," I said. "Nutmeg smells good."

"You made me feel like a loser, Roo," he said. "Like a complete outsider."

Shiv, the golden, the popular, the perfect. Saying this to me.

"I didn't say what you thought I said," I whispered. "At least, I didn't mean what you thought I meant."

"Okay, then," he said.

"I liked you. They were asking me what it was like to kiss you. That's all. It's how girls are, together. No one said anything bad."

"All right."

"The gross thing was about ear licking. Cricket asked if we did ear licking, and I'd never heard of it before."

He laughed a little. "I guess that's nice to know."

"All this time I thought it was something wrong with me that made you stop talking to me," I said.

"It was," he pointed out.

"I mean with my kissing, or my body, or my personality."

"It was your personality."

"Oh." I tried to crack a smile. "But it was a mistake. Please believe me. I would never say that stuff about you."[2]

"Yeah, okay."

"The Indian thing is not a thing. I mean . . ."

---

[2] When I think about it, this is both true and not true. I have talked a lot of trash about people. Meghan. Hutch. Katarina. I really have. But throughout this whole horror, I never said one mean thing about Kim, Cricket or Nora to anyone, even when all that stuff was up on the bathroom wall.

So am I a bad person or a good person?

"I got it, Roo."

"I'm all messed up now."

"Yeah, well. I'm all messed up too," he said. "But thanks for the explanation."

He hiked his bag over his shoulder and walked down to the parking lot without offering me a ride.

13. Jackson (Yes, okay, he was my boyfriend. Don't ask me any more about it.)

By now, you know everything about Jackson Clarke, probably way more than anyone on earth wants to hear. This is all I have to add:

I still think about him every day.

When I see him, my heart jumps up in my chest.

I long for him to talk to me, and whenever he even says hello, I feel a thousand times worse than I did before.

I wish he was dead.

I wish he still liked me.

●

When I got home from talking to Shiv, Hutch was on my deck. Again. Wednesday and Sunday afternoons, he helps my dad greenhouse the southern deck. Especially now that the weather's good, the two of them are always huddled together over a peony bush or a broken windowpane, the boom box blasting cassette tapes of Hutch's retro metal.

The sunlight was starting to fade; it was maybe six o'clock. "Hey, Hutch. Hey, Dad," I called, waving as I came down the dock. The two of them were staring up at the greenhouse, which I had to admit was coming together. "You guys taking a break?"

My dad had taken to hiding Popsicles in the way-back of the freezer, so that he and I could get enough calories in the macrobiotic nightmare of our life. I popped inside and got one for me, one for my dad and one for Hutch, too (my mother was out, needless to say). Then the three of us sat on the edge of the deck, leaning forward so the Popsicles didn't melt on our clothes, watching the boats sail across the lake.

I actually felt happy for the first time since Jackson broke up with me.

Now don't go getting excited that I'll suddenly notice Hutch in the soft pink light of the sunset and fall in love. He's *not* the love of my life, and no, we *haven't* been destined to get together ever since those gummy bears back in fourth grade, just because that's what happens in movies.[1] And don't go thinking he and I become best

---

[1] Movies where the apparently hopeless dorky guy who's been there all along eventually gets the girl: *The Wedding Singer. Dumb and Dumber. When Harry Met Sally. There's Something About Mary. Beauty and the Beast. While You Were Sleeping. Revenge of the Nerds.* Lots of Woody Allen movies.

friends in a *Breakfast Club* sort of way, either,[2] with me realizing he's got a heart of gold under the Iron Maiden motorcycle jacket, and him realizing that I'm not the slut everyone thinks I am. Yes, that happens onscreen. But forget it. This is real life. He creeps me out. We have nothing in common besides leprosy.

"Roo, good to see you looking cheerful," said my dad. "Isn't it nice to see her cheerful, John? It's been taking her a while to process her feelings about the breakup with Jackson. He was her first serious boyfriend, you know."

"You're better off without that guy," said Hutch, his mouth full of Popsicle.

"You think so?" I said. "I don't."

"He's a jerk."

"Huh?"

"Not a nice guy, Roo. He's mean inside."

"Why do you say that?"

Then Hutch told this story. I'm not sure why he told it, except that he and my dad had been doing some heavy manly rocker bonding. Or maybe he felt sorry for me, even though I was such a bitch to him most of the time. Hutch said that he and Jackson had been friends in sixth grade–the year when, at Tate, you start moving from room to room for each class instead of staying all day in one place with one teacher. Jackson was a year ahead, but they had gym together, and French, and the same free

---

[2] *The Breakfast Club:* Movie where popular kids and lepers all get detention together and learn to appreciate each other's inner beauty and personal differences.

periods—so they started hanging out. As a sixth grader, Hutch was friends with all the cool seventh-grade boys: Kyle, Matt, Jackson and a few others. They played kickball after school. They had their own table in the refectory. They made a lot of noise in the hallways. Jackson and Hutch were friends in particular: Hutch used to ride his bike over to Jackson's house on weekends, and Jackson stayed at Hutch's when his parents had to go to Tokyo on business one week. When the two of them were bored in class, they'd write funny rhymes about the teachers and stick them in each other's mail cubbies.

Mean Madame Long,
I know I got the answers wrong.
You can sit me on the bench,
You can call me "stupid wench,"
You can raise a giant stench,
But I can't remember French.

That kind of thing. That's the one he recited for us. Anyway, summer came, and Hutch went off traveling for most of it with his family, and when he got back in seventh (when Jackson was in eighth), he found himself frozen out. "I got zits over the summer," he said to me and my dad, staring down at his Popsicle stick. "I looked like hell, and I was still completely short. And they'd all been to sports camp together while I'd been away.

"First week of school, I trailed after them, sitting on one end of our table, not much part of the talk. Still showing up for kickball. Something seemed off, but I couldn't tell what. These guys were my friends, you know?

"Then one day, I wrote a rhyme about Mr. Krell–remember, the middle-school gym teacher? And I stuck it in Jackson's cubby like we did the year before."[3]

"Oh man," said my dad. "I can see it coming. Children can be so cruel."

"I got my same note back with something scrawled across the top in Jackson's writing," Hutch went on. " 'Joke's long over. Loser.' " He stood up and tossed his Popsicle stick in the trash can.

"That's all it said?" I asked.

" 'Joke's long over. Loser.' "

"Wow."

"He never talked to me again. Like we'd never been friends. Like we'd never even met. And when Kyle and those guys filled my locker with ball bearings in eighth,[4] and they poured out all over the floor–Jackson didn't say a word. Just stood there, changing his shirt like nothing was even happening."

"Jackson would never do that," I said.

---

[3] A couple of days after this conversation, I asked Hutch what the Krell rhyme was, Mr. Krell being this enthusiastic blond man with pink cheeks who really was a most tempting subject for ridicule. Hutch still remembers it, so here it is:
Mister Krell, oh, how you smell!
I think it must be aftershave!
The smell gets stronger every day.
Our gym is sinking in a wave
Of Krell's old smelly aftershave.
Mr. Krell, why don't you wait,
And wear that stuff out on a date?
[4] A locker full of heavy metal. Ha ha ha.

"Well, he did. Who knows?" Hutch shrugged. "He might have put the bearings in himself."

"No way."

"I'm just telling you what happened."

"He's not like that anymore," I said. "If he ever was."

"Dream on," said Hutch. And then, like he was singing: "Dream on!"

"Dream on!"[5] squeaked my dad, in a stupid rock 'n' roll falsetto.

Hutch joined him, and they kept squealing "dream on" like stuck pigs until, simultaneously, they yelled, "Dream-a make-a dream come true!"[6] They both sang, and stopped for a little air-guitar duet.

With this additional evidence of (1) Hutch's creepy tendency to make references to antique heavy metal songs that no one else knows about and (2) my dad actually knowing them and liking it and (3) a complete lack of dignity on both their parts, the moment was over. No more sharing was going to happen. My dad hit Play on the old cassette deck, and the entire dock of houseboats was bombarded with retro metal.

Was Jackson truly the kind of guy who would fill someone's locker with ball bearings? Or even just stand there, saying nothing, when his friends were humiliating someone? Had he really written "Joke's long over. Loser"

---

[5] *Dream On:* I asked my dad. It's a song by Aerosmith, from way back when they didn't have any wrinkles.

[6] That's what it sounded like.

on that poem? It didn't seem like the kind of thing Hutch could invent.

But it didn't seem like the guy I knew, either.

Maybe Jackson had done those things but wasn't that way anymore. We all grow up and regret the mean things we did in middle school.

Or maybe I never knew him that well in the first place.

I grabbed my bike, rode to the nearest store (ten blocks) and bought two large bunches of basil, a box of pasta, walnuts and a wedge of Parmesan cheese. Then I boiled noodles and made pesto sauce in our blender, before my mom got back to tell me it wasn't macrobiotic.

●

The next morning, in the Jeep, I asked Meghan if she wanted to go to the movies. I felt like I was inviting her on a date. A Woody Allen festival was playing at the Variety.

"Can I bring Bick?" she asked, honking her horn at some idiot driving an SUV.

"No. I think it's a girl thing." I didn't want to be a third wheel with Meghan and her boyfriend.

"We're supposed to go over to Steve's house and shoot pool on Saturday."

"Oh."

"But I don't want to go. Those guys are always drinking beer and nobody talks to me," she said. And then to the drive-thru window: "Two vanilla cappuccinos, grande." And then to me: "It's not that fun. I usually go out on the porch by myself, actually."

"So blow him off."

She didn't say anything for a minute. We paid for the cappuccinos and she pulled out into traffic. "Yeah. Okay. I can see him Friday."

"It's a plan, then?"

"Uh-huh."

We might be friends.

14. Noel (but it was just a rumor.)

My mom decided to go on tour with her one-woman show.[1] The producer said she could still book it, even though the Seattle run had ended in October, so *Elaine Oliver: Twist and Shout* would be going around the country starting the end of next month (June). My dad was upset, but my mom said, "Kevin, I have to give the public what it wants. Besides, we can use the money to go on vacation in August."

"You can't leave Roo."

"Oh, she's a big girl."

---

[1] The part about Noel is at the end of the chapter. I have to write down this other important stuff first.

"She's a *teenage* girl. She needs her mother around."

"Dad, I'm standing right here."

"Will you miss me, Roo?" asked my mom.

"She will!" cried my dad. "Even if she won't admit it."

"Not that much," I said. "You should go."

"She can come with me, Kevin. After finals."

There was no way I was spending the summer watching *Twist and Shout* every night and living in hotel rooms. "It'll be fun," my mom went on. "I'm going to San Francisco in July."

"Elaine."

"Kevin."

"Elaine."

"What? It'll be good for her. She's never been anywhere except summer camp."

"Didn't we go over this before?" sighed my dad. "We decided you wouldn't go on tour unless I could go with you, and Roo could stay with Grandma Suzette." (Grandma Suzette, my father's mother, lives nearby. But she was scheduled for foot surgery, so I couldn't stay with her.)

"I changed my mind," snapped my mom. "I refuse to stay here and watch you greenhouse every weekend when gay men all across the nation are clamoring to see my show. They even have Elaine Oliver T-shirts in San Francisco; some fans sent me a photograph."

"That was three years ago."

"Which is why it's time to go back."

"Dad," I whispered, loud enough for Mom to hear. "When she's gone, we can eat anything we want."

"Two months is a long time," he said. "Let me think about it."

"It's done," snapped my mother. "Ricki booked it yesterday."

My dad stormed out and spent the rest of the evening hammering away on the greenhouse.

I had no interest in going on tour with my mother. Zero. None. To my way of thinking, it would be a complete waste; she'd be yapping in my ear all the time, feeding me tofu, demanding that I bond with her and never listening to a word I say. I'd have to see her show every night, and have theater managers pinch my cheeks and say, "Oh, Ruby! I've heard all about you. It seems like only yesterday your mother was doing that bit about your first menstrual period!" We'd sit in hotel rooms, night after night, watching television, when we could be sitting on the dock in the warm air. I'd miss swimming in the lake, and biking across town, and Meghan had said something about taking me out in her family's motorboat. I'd miss the painting class I'd signed up for. I'd even miss seeing my father's garden bloom, and the bumblebees that practically surround our houseboat every summer.

But then, one afternoon, I was coming out of Mr. Wallace's office after meeting with him about my final H&P paper. I had stopped in the hallway to put my stuff in my backpack, and a voice I recognized said, "Ruby Oliver. Long time."

It was Gideon Van Deusen. Him with his lovely hairy eyebrows. Back from his cross-country tour.

He was wearing a peace sign T-shirt and a beaded belt. Sunglasses. His hair was longer than last time I'd seen him. He sat down on the bench next to me. "What are you doing here?" I asked.

"What, no 'Nice to see you, Gideon'? No, 'How you been, Gideon?' Just 'What are you doing here?' That's no kind of greeting."

"Oh. Um. Sorry, I–" How could I be such a jerk?

"I'm teasing you, Ruby," he said, laughing. "I need an extra recommendation for Evergreen from Mr. Wallace. There's this advanced-level history class I want to take and they're making me get one."

"When did you get back?"

"Last week. Didn't Nora tell you?"

I looked down at the floor.

"Or are you two still in a snit?" Gideon smiled.

"Me and almost everyone, actually."

"She wrote me something like that in an e-mail. But Nora misses you. I know she does."

"I doubt it."

"She didn't say anything directly," Gideon admitted. "She's just home a lot, lounging around. Messing with her Instamatic. Shooting baskets in the driveway by herself. Kim and Cricket are all in love, you know. Always out with the boys."

"Yeah, I know." I had honestly never thought about what Nora was doing when the rest of us were out with our boyfriends.

"You should call her."

"Maybe." I shrugged.

We sat there for a minute. I fiddled with the zipper on my backpack.

"I was in Big Sur last month," Gideon said, finally. "You know where that is? South of San Francisco, along the coast. They have hot springs there, hot water bubbling up from underground, and you go in without any clothes, men and women together, lounging around naked with steam rising up.[2] And I'm learning to surf."

"Cool."

"You need a wet suit that far north. It's cold. But I kept at it and now I can stand up and catch a wave pretty damn good, if I say so myself."

"Wow."

"You would love it. You're a swimmer, right?"

"Yeah."

"So you'd be good at it. You have that upper-body strength. Then I drove up to San Francisco," he went on. "And I heard some awesome bands. You been there?"

"No."

"It's amazing. The wildest people walking through the streets. Men in drag. I did an open-mike night with my guitar at this coffeehouse. I pretty much sucked, but I got out in front of people and actually sang, can you believe it?"

"Good for you, rock star."

"Well." He laughed. "I felt like a goofball. But hey, I'm never seeing any of those people again, so what the hell?"

---

[2] The next minute of the conversation is not written down with any accuracy. I wasn't paying attention, because I was too busy picturing Gideon naked in a hot spring full of steam.

"Exactly." It was very un–Tommy Hazard, getting up and singing badly in front of a crowd, but somehow it made me like Gideon even more.

"I never would have done something like that at Tate," he said. "When I was here, my whole world was just sports, and parties, and refectory gossip. The Tate universe."

"Yeah." I knew all about the Tate universe.

"I'm serious," Gideon said. "Chinese food like you've never eaten. Architecture. Landscapes. Before I came west, I was in the desert in Arizona. I saw the Great Lakes. I hiked some of the Appalachian Trail."

Mr. Wallace cracked his door and stuck his head out into the hallway. "Van Deusen!" he cried, his face lighting up. "Slumming, are you?" He ushered Gideon in.

I was late for my next class, but I walked there slowly. Thinking about Gideon, naked in the hot spring.

And about San Francisco.

●

People in general are bad apologizers. Even my dad is—for all his talk about forgiveness. He doesn't say sorry. He grabs my mom from behind and starts kissing her neck.

"Kevin, I'm still mad at you," she complains.

"Oh, but you smell good," he whispers into her throat.

"Kevin!"

"No one smells as good as you," he moans, or some other ridiculousness, and before long she says, "Fine. Come look at this thing I bought today," or something like that.

Mom is even worse. She sulks and pouts and storms around the house banging pots and pans, and then after a couple of hours she starts acting like everything's okay again, and Dad and I are supposed to know that she's over whatever it was and not to mention it again.

Other people apologize and don't mean it. "Sorry, but you shouldn't have . . ." or "Sorry, but I just didn't . . ." They apologize while telling you that they were right all along, which is the opposite of an actual apology.

I am definitely a bad apologizer. I talk too much. I leave the whole thing until way too late, and then I babble on, and end up not saying what I mean and starting whatever argument it was over again. It never comes out right.

Well, truth be told, I usually still think the other person was wrong, and that's probably why.

The next Thursday, Doctor Z looked down at the list and asked me about Noel. "It was only a rumor," I said. "About me and him. One of forty-eight rumors, by this point."

"He's the one you held hands with at the party?"

"Yeah. He stands on the other side of the studio in Painting Elective now. I never even talk to him."

"And?"

"I don't know. I don't even think he likes girls."

"Why not?"

"He's a mystery."

"You don't have feelings for him?"

"It doesn't matter, even if I did. I told him to fuck off. It's not like he'd ever talk to me again."

Doctor Z paused in her know-it-all way, like she was

waiting for me to say something. I didn't. "Why is he on your list?" she finally asked.

"Do we even need the list anymore?" I asked back. "I mean, what are we going to talk about once it's finished?"

"That's up to you."

"I knew you'd say that."

Silence.

"So why *is* he on your list?" she finally asked.

The thing is, I liked Noel. He was interesting. He was different. He was outside the Tate universe, at least a little bit. When he took me home after the Spring Fling and held my hand at the party, it felt good. I liked talking to him.

The Sunday after Meghan and I went to the Woody Allen festival,[3] I dug my watercolor paints out of the very bottom of my desk drawer. I don't think I had used them on my own since seventh grade. I got a piece of white paper and folded it in half. "How am I sorry?" I wrote in purple watercolor. "Let me count the ways . . ."

And inside, I wrote:

1. Like a shark who ate a license plate by mistake.
2. Like a movie star caught without her makeup.
3. Like a lady with a fancy hairdo, in the rain without an umbrella.
4. Like a cat who rolled in jam.
5. Like a hungry raccoon that ate its young by mistake.
6. Like a neurotic teenage girl, traumatized by recent

---

[3] The movie we saw, *Everything You Always Wanted to Know About Sex But Were Afraid to Ask,* involves a superenormous breast chasing people across the countryside. They finally capture it in a giant bra.

social debacles, who doesn't know a friend when he looks her in the eye, and gives her a ride home, and offers to ruin his reputation for her.

I painted a tiny picture of each person/animal with deep remorse on its face. The last one was me, down in the bottom corner.

It took me a couple of hours, but it looked pretty good when I was done—although the raccoon and the cat were pretty similar, and the rain didn't seem very rainy. I blew off my Bio/Sex Ed lab, Geometry worksheet and Brit Lit reading to finish it.

The next morning, I put it in Noel's mail cubby, feeling embarrassed, but also rather well adjusted, if I do say so myself.

I figured I wouldn't see him until Painting in the afternoon, and I had no idea what to say to him when I did, or whether I should try to put my easel next to his, or what. But I actually got in line right behind him at lunchtime,[4] and he was in the middle of negotiating with the lunch lady about whether she'd be willing to put his slice of pizza in the microwave (she was claiming it was hot enough; he was saying it was cold), and he barely even looked at me, and I almost turned around and snuck back out the door of the refectory—but then he reached out and grabbed my hand and squeezed it, and held it all the while

---

[4] I'd been lying low, generally. No fishnets. No wild clothes. At lunch, I was sitting with Meghan and the seniors. Most of the older kids ignored me, except for Bick, who was pretty cool. But I was definitely still a leper. Hutch and I did say hi in the halls now, and the girls from lacrosse were perfectly civil, like if I had a question about schoolwork, or practice or something. But that was it.

he was doing this monologue about the difference in texture between cold mozzarella and hot, while the lunch lady looked at him with murder in her eyes.

He lost the argument, let go of my hand with a final squeeze, took his chilly pizza and went out into the dining hall to sit with a table of freshman girls I'd never noticed before.

I felt like I was walking on air.

15. Cabbie (but I'm undecided.)

It seems weird to me now that Cabbie is even on the Boyfriend List, although it's true we went on an actual date and there was even physical contact of a strangely advanced nature.

I've already pretty much forgotten about him. I'm certainly not undecided about him anymore. Shep Cabot is out, finished, kaput—and the heading of this chapter should more accurately read: "Cabbie (but it was just a grope.)"

Cabbie is a junior. He plays rugby and he's cute in a meaty sort of way. He's not my type. Too big. Too manly manly. He caught up with me after a lacrosse game a couple of days after the Spring Fling and asked me to the movies. Out of the blue. Right before my first appointment with Doctor Z. My guess is, he'd heard I was easy[1] thanks to Mr. Wallace's well-publicized antislut lecture in H&P, and he figured he could get some if he paid for my movie ticket.[2]

I didn't much care *why* he was asking me out.

I didn't want to sit home on Friday night.

I wanted Jackson to see me with someone else—like he had with Angelo—and feel jealous, and want me back.

I wanted not to care if Jackson wanted me back or not, because I had a new guy who was bigger and more popular and played rugby.

And once I didn't care and was off with the new guy, Jackson would suddenly love me—wouldn't he?

And then I could care again and we'd live happily ever after.[3]

I said yes, and Cabbie picked me up in a BMW around seven p.m. on Friday night. He came in, briefly, and shook my dad's hand and called him sir. We drove to the University District, where there are a couple of movie theaters, and parked in an expensive lot. "Can't leave this baby on the street," said Cabbie, chuckling, as he locked the doors. We walked a couple of blocks in the chilly air, talking about lacrosse and rugby.

"We're playing Sullivan on Tuesday," said Cabbie. "You should come to the game."

---

[1] Doctor Z: "Is it impossible that he liked you as a person and just wanted to go to the movies with you?"

Me: "Yes."

[2] And he was right! Ag.

[3] Complete idiocy. I know.

"That could be cool."

"Coach is such a hard-ass. He's making us run three miles before practice."

"We run three for lacrosse, too."

"Really, the girls?"

"Really."

"I'm starting this season, which is cool."

"Awesome."

We went into the theater. He bought the tickets. I paid for popcorn and pop. It was some action special-effects movie, not my thing, but all right.

About a quarter into it, Cabbie put his arm around me, and seconds later, he dangled his right hand down over my shoulder and squeezed my boob! We hadn't held hands, or kissed, or anything. We'd hardly even had a conversation before that night–but he went straight for the boob squeeze as if it was the most normal thing in the world.

I was in shock. I sat there, letting him squeeze it.

It felt kind of good.

He was watching the movie like it wasn't even happening, but also moving his fingers around every now and then, stroking my boob absentmindedly.

Should I shift my body so his hand was more shoulder height? Or take his hand and hold it so it couldn't go roaming around my chest? Or actively move his arm back to his lap? Or get up to go to the bathroom and hope the gropefest wouldn't start up again when I got back? Or pitch a fit and get all indignant?

It really did feel kind of good. He seemed to know

what he was doing in the boob department. The longer I sat there and thought about it, the longer it seemed weird to start objecting.

He ended up feeling my boob for the whole movie! He ate popcorn with his left hand and got lucky with his right. It started to feel kind of lopsided, for the right one to get literally an hour and a half's worth of attention and the left one to be all on its lonesome. I barely knew what the movie was about, because I was thinking about my boob the whole time. My boob, being stroked by a near-complete stranger, a big meaty rugby player.

When eight days before, it had been all Jackson's.

Was I really a slut, like Kim said? This made four boys within one week I'd had some kind of physical contact with.[4]

Or did I actually like Cabbie? Could this be the start of a new thing?

Maybe not.

And then again, maybe.

The movie ended. Cabbie stretched, took his hand off me and stood up. "Wanna get some pizza?"

"Sure."

We went to a place up the street. We split a cheese pie. He told me he doesn't eat vegetables, ever. He talked about his "buddies" from rugby and how he wants to go to Penn and be a lawyer, like his dad. He asked me about my family, and I did my usual riff. He said his mother likes to garden.

---

[4] In case you don't remember: Jackson, Noel, Angelo and Cabbie.

Cabbie had everything a girl is supposed to look for in a boy. He was sporty, cute, popular, friendly, rich. He might even have been smart, though I couldn't tell for sure.

But I was bored. Just making conversation, not really talking.

I think I want a guy who eats vegetables.

And who isn't so normal.

He was just a muffin, you know?

The check took forever to come, and when it finally did, I insisted on paying half, even though I was still broke from buying that silver dress.

He drove me home and I hopped out of the car like a jackrabbit. If he thought I was a slut, who knows what he was expecting in a dark BMW, late on a Friday night? Especially after all that boob squeezing. "That was fun," I lied, slamming the car door. "You don't have to walk me in."

"Later," he said, looking surprised.

Sunday evening I called him up. "Hey, Cabbie," I said, when he got to the phone. "I want to tell you, um, I can't go to that rugby game on Tuesday."

"That's cool. We play all the time. There's another game on Friday."

"Yeah, well. I mean, I'm kind of still getting over Jackson."

"Oh," he said. "That's cool."

"All right. Well, sorry about that."

"No big deal. See you around."

"See you."

We hung up. I felt relieved. Although if I could have had a purely boob-squeezing relationship with him, maybe I would have done that. You know, like sitting in movie theaters once or twice a week having my boobs groped, with no obligation to kiss his meaty face or have boring conversations with the guy.

But that was impossible, so we were better off apart.

The next day was the day Kim Xeroxed the Boyfriend List and put it in everyone's mail cubbies. My life was sucking in all the ways I've already detailed, and on top of it all I heard Cabbie saying to Billy Alexander, "Yeah, I felt her up. But I don't know, she's kind of skanky. I'm not so interested. What about you?"

"Don't look at me, man," Billy said.

"Come on, you can tell me."

"I'm serious man, I didn't touch her."

"Nice tits, though, am I right?"[5]

"Sure."

"Was it Billy *Krespin,* then, do you think?" asked Cabbie.

"Could be. Why don't you ask him?"

And that was that. You know the rest.

The good thing about the whole Cabbie episode was that I realized I might actually like having my body touched by somebody other than Jackson. I mean, being

---

[5] I wanted to kill him. Telling another guy how he squeezed my boob! What a sleazy gross thing to say. But now, I think it's not so different from what I told my friends about Shiv and Jackson, and what I know about Kaleb and Finn and Pete.

felt up[6] is pretty intimate, and before going out with Cabbie I thought I'd never want to do anything like that with anyone ever again.

It did feel good, I can't lie about that.

Maybe I won't be heartbroken forever.

●

Doctor Z and I are done with the list. Now we just have conversations. She gave me another homework assignment, which was to make a drawing of my family, and I ended up making this little diorama of our houseboat, using an old shoe box. It came out pretty cool. I had this little cutout of my mom waving her arms, and one of my dad hugging a peony bush, and one of me, wearing fishnets.

I've started wearing the fishnets again.

Doctor Z thinks it's a healthy expression of my sexuality.

I just think they look good.

Other than that, I tell her about my life. I haven't had any more panic attacks, although sometimes my heart races and I do a little deep breathing. "Do I get a clean bill of health now?" I asked her.

"What do you think?" Ag. She really does make me insane with that kind of question.

"Um. I don't know."

"Would you *like* a clean bill of health?"

---

[6] Or actually *down*, in this case, given that his hand was coming from over my shoulder.

I sighed. "I don't want to be a mental patient forever."

"Are you saying you'd like to stop therapy, Ruby?"

"Um."

"You don't have to stop until you want to. We can do this as long as you like."

"Don't you get bored, listening to my problems?"

"No."

"You probably have a bunch of anorexics and sex addicts who are a lot more interesting."

"It's not your job to entertain me, Ruby."

True enough. That's why therapists are different from friends. You don't have to make them like you.

So I kept going.

I guess I like it.

School is over now. Jackson and Kim are still together. He doesn't seem to have realized he loves me. In fact, he seems to have forgotten everything that happened. Neither of them spoke to me the rest of the year except for Jackson saying hello when absolutely necessary—and I still had the Beth-Ann-Courtney-Heidi-Kim radar all through the very last day of finals, stupid as that is. People still whispered about me in the hall, but no one wrote anything more on the bathroom wall. I kept my head down. I hung out with Noel in Painting Elective and ate lunch with Meghan. Once, after a game, I went for ice cream with a crowd of girls from the lacrosse team. I haven't been back to the B&O.

You might think that Heidi started going with Finn the stud-muffin, since he took her to the Spring Fling as a Kim replacement. But it didn't work out that way. Heidi's now dating Tommy Parrish, who used to go out with Cricket.

Ariel and Shiv are still together, but I heard her in the locker room saying she thought Steve Buchannon (Bick's friend) was completely hot. Cricket and Pete split up. Pete started going out with Katarina–until Katarina made out with the Whipper at yet another party I wasn't invited to, and Pete got mad and broke up with her. So now she's going out with Cabbie. And Pete is going out with Courtney. And Finn is going out with Beth. Cricket started dating Billy Alexander, which I'm sure she's cranked about since she's lusted for him ever since that one time he drove her home from that basketball game. But he also just graduated, and I don't know the whole story, because we don't talk.

It's still the Tate universe.

I ran into Nora in the University District right after school ended. I had been shopping for a bathing suit, and I had just left the store when she called my name from across the street. I showed her what I'd bought. She liked it.

We talked about tan lines, and how the bathing suits that make nice tan lines aren't the ones you look good in, somehow. She said her boobs get squashed flat or pushed up, and why wasn't there a bathing suit that made boobs just look normal? You would think scientists and fashion designers could have figured that out by now.

It was good to see her. She wasn't up to much, she said. Watching TV. Hanging out with Gideon a little. Her mom had bought her a new camera, a real one where you have to adjust everything.

I felt like guilting her for cutting me out all spring, but I thought about something Doctor Z said, which was that sometimes it's a good idea to think about what you *want* from a situation, and try to get it, rather than just blurt out the first thing that comes into your head. And I realized I was glad Nora was talking to me, finally—and I didn't want to mess it up. So I said, "Hey, I love your brother again."

"He's got a girlfriend," she said. "Diana. She's a poet."

"I know," I answered, although I didn't really. "But he just does it for me, anyhow."

She laughed. "There's no accounting for taste."

"I'm through with boys for the moment, anyway," I said. "Too dangerous."

"Yeah."

"I mean, it can get ugly out there."

"Uh-huh. I think it's better as a spectator sport."

"What, dating?"

"Uh-huh." Nora scratched her neck. "It's just so messy, you know, all that stuff with you and Kim and Heidi and—"

"I got you."

"I just feel like, I'd rather shoot baskets, or some-thing," she went on. "Even read a book. I mean, not that there's anyone I'm into, anyway."

"The problem is," I joked, "our school is too damn small. Remember how we wrote that in *The Boy Book?* Any decent boy was used up ages ago."

"I don't know," she muttered. "Sometimes I feel like a leper."

That surprised me almost as much as Shiv Neel,

golden boy, thinking we were all laughing at him because he was Indian.

Like even the people at the center of the Tate universe feel like they're on the outside.

Nora said she was late, hoisted her bag over her shoulder and waved goodbye. I watched her go down the street and get into her car.

Maybe I'll give her a call later in the summer, when the whole debacle is a bit more behind us.

Maybe.

I slept over at Meghan's house a couple of nights in June. She has a huge bathroom all to herself and two twin beds and a collection of like forty different perfumes. I found out she's still a virgin, though she lets Bick go down on her.[7]

My dad is still working on the greenhouse. It's coming along.

Here is what I think about these days: Jackson. Pitiful, but true. The ceramic frogs are still sitting on my dresser,

---

[7] Me: "You *let* him? Isn't that supposed to be fun for *you*?"

Her: "It's supposed to be, but I get bored."

"How come?"

"I don't know, it's just boring. Maybe he's not very good at it."

"What's it like?"

"Not much. Not like in the sex-ed books. I think about other stuff while he's doing it."

"Why bother, then?"

"I don't know." She shrugged. "It's something to do. I think it makes him feel like a sex god."

"Maybe you could train him. So he'd get better at it."

"Maybe. I hate to burst his little sex god bubble. He seems so proud of himself, after."

with a photograph of the two of us holding hands out on my deck. I think he may not be the nicest person, really. He's not the person I thought he was. Some days, I'm mad at him, actually—which I wasn't before. For the bad presents, and the forgotten phone calls, for the stupid anime movies. And for Kim. But that happens in waves, on certain days. The other days, I think about the lollipop-tasting experiment, and kissing in my kitty-cat suit—and I feel like I lost something.

I'd probably still take him back, if he showed up at my door like in the movies.

He's Jackson Clarke.

It's just how I feel.

I think about Cricket and Nora. And how much I used to laugh. And how I'd go into the refectory in the morning and they'd be sitting there, drinking tea (Cricket) and Diet Coke (Nora) and goofing around (Kim was always late), and how that was the best part of my day, most days—and how it'll never happen again.

And of course, I think about Kim. It's so weird that I used to have a best friend and now I don't. I have a drawer full of pictures of her. The red vintage jacket she bought me for my birthday is hanging in my closet, and the book about Salvador Dalí I borrowed is sitting on my desk. I've got *The Boy Book* on the shelf in my bedroom where it's always been, a big, ratty notebook with our handwriting all over it. I even thought about photocopying it and mailing it to her as a kind of reproach. Or maybe as a gesture of friendship. I'm not sure which.

But I didn't.

I still automatically pick up the phone to call her when something happens that's worth talking about, then remember and put the phone down again without dialing. Sometimes I call Meghan instead–but most of the time, I don't call anyone. Doctor Z told me I'm going through a "grieving process," and that all these behaviors are natural.

I told her that phrases like "grieving process" make me gag.

She laughed and said it's still a process and it's still grieving, whatever I want to call it.

I said let's call it Reginald. "I'm doing Reginald today," I say now, when I'm feeling like I have no friends.

I think about Angelo, too, which is deeply perverse because he probably doesn't ever want to talk to me again (subject of much therapy discussion). My family went to dinner at Juana's again in May, but he wasn't there. He sort of lives in a different universe–not the Tate universe– and I wonder sometimes what it's like. Why he asked me to the Homecoming dance. Why he came to the party and brought me that corsage. What he thinks of that dog-filled house. What he does after school. Whether he's thinking about college. What he looks like without a shirt.

I think about books. I read through a stack of paperback mystery novels from the public library when the term ended, and then I read some books from Brit Lit that I blew off during the year. I watch too many movies. I think I've seen all the Woody Allens now.

I think about getting a job. No more babysitting. I hate it. Maybe I could help out at the Woodland Park Zoo for a few bucks an hour. Or at the library.

I think about getting my driver's license. Not that I'd have a car, but I could take the Honda on weekends, maybe. My birthday is in August. I'll be sixteen.

I think about turning sixteen, and how I won't have a party like I always thought I would, with my friends all sleeping over and being silly and eating cake.

I probably think too much.

In early July, I got on my first ever airplane and went to join my mom in San Francisco, where she's doing her show. I didn't want to go, I said I'd rather rot than hang out with her all summer, and my dad made a lot more fuss about her being selfish and how that wasn't how they'd agreed to run their marriage—but in the end, she went— and I realized I wanted to go too. I wanted to see some

men in drag and some general California stuff and just go somewhere where the air smells different. I called her up when she was in Los Angeles and asked if I could come meet her in San Francisco. It was funny. I didn't think I'd be as glad to see her as I was when she picked me up at the airport. When we're done here, we're going to Chicago and Minneapolis.

Don't get me wrong. Elaine Oliver is driving me nuts, because I have to share her hotel room and she is so full of self-importance, what with an audience clapping for her every night, that she's damn near impossible to deal with— but she's given up the macrobiotic thing and she took me to five different Chinese restaurants for lunch, all in one week. They have an amazing Chinatown here. It feels like you're in a different country.

When she's doing her show, I stay in the hotel and write on her laptop–which is the stuff you're reading now. Or I mess around with my watercolors. Or read more mysteries. Then I fall asleep and she comes home and calls my dad and moans about how much she misses him, which wakes me up. And then I talk to her while she takes off all her makeup.

In the daytime, we go do tourist stuff. I saw the Golden Gate Bridge, rode a streetcar, toured Alcatraz. We walked through the Castro district, where someone asked my mom for an autograph.

Last Monday, the day when theaters are dark, we rented a car and drove down the coast to see Big Sur. I drove part of the way, and when my mother commented eight times about how fast I was changing lanes and had I checked whether I was going the speed limit, I told her to please be quiet for at least fifteen minutes and see if we stayed alive. And she did.

At one point we stopped and took a picnic down to the beach. It was cold, and sand got in our potato salad, but we stayed anyway. There were surfers in the water, looking like seals in their wet suits, sailing into shore on huge waves. We watched them for like an hour.

Tommy Hazard would have loved it.

I loved it.

I was out of the Tate universe, standing on the edge of the sea.

the boyfriend list

e. lockhart

(15 guys, 11 shrink appointments, 4 ceramic frogs and me, ruby oliver)

A READERS GUIDE

1. After the Adam "debacle" in chapter one, Roo and Kim begin a notebook called *The Boy Book* in which they write down everything they know about boys. Have you ever started a book like this on your own or with your friends? Do you think it would be useful? What information would you include?

2. On page 41, Ruby spills her guts to Kim about Finn. Is this smart? Are there circumstances in which it's better to keep your mouth shut? Has something like this ever happened to you—you tried to do the right thing and it backfired?

3. Ruby gives three examples of the way love works in the movies. In her example on page 64, the couples hate each other half the time but still get together in the end. In her example on page 65, the couple breaks up, but then the man realizes that he loves the woman and can't exist without her, and they get back together and live happily ever after. And on page 198, the hopeless dorky guy who's been there all along eventually gets the girl. Do you agree with Ruby that these happy endings don't happen in real life? Pick one of the movies mentioned and discuss it. Does the romantic situation in the movie ring true? Can you think of other movies, books, or television shows that would fit on Ruby's lists?

4. Ruby discovers that dating Jackson isn't the way she thought dating was supposed to be. Have you ever discovered that your ideas about something were wrong? How was the reality different from what you had imagined?

5. In chapter six, Kim and Ruby invent the perfect boyfriend and name him Tommy Hazard. Do you have your own Tommy Hazard? Are there hazards in creating a "perfect" boyfriend?

6. After stealing Jackson, Kim tells Ruby, "When you find your Tommy Hazard you'll understand. I honestly couldn't help it." Do you agree with Kim's justification of her behavior? Does she do the right thing?

7. Even though Noel has become Roo's only ally, she turns on him on page 176 after he says, ". . . if those are your friends you've got no need for enemies." Why does this upset Ruby so much? Do you think Noel is right? Why is Ruby not yet ready to give up her old life, even though it has become the source of such pain?

8. When Kim calls Ruby a slut in class, Mr. Wallace gives a lecture on the negative effects of labels and points out that "there are no equivalent epithets for men whatsoever, and didn't *that* say something about how women are viewed in our culture?" (page 177). What *does* it say? Can you give examples of the negative effects of labels, from real life or from movies, music, television shows, or books?

9. Ruby ends the book by saying, "I was out of the Tate universe, standing on the edge of the sea" (page 229). What does she mean by this? Is she really out of the Tate universe? Is this a satisfying ending? Do you believe that Ruby is in a better place now than when the book began? What do you think is next for her?

in her own words

a conversation with e. lockhart

Q. Where did you get the idea for *The Boyfriend List*? Did you have a boyfriend list?

A. In high school, I used to keep a list of all the boys I ever kissed. There were little hearts dotting the *i*s and everything! But when I looked for it some fifteen years after graduating, the list had disappeared.

I hoped it hadn't fallen into the wrong hands.

And there was an idea.

It was quite a difficult book to structure, in the end. After all, a list is not a story, and with the list structure I had to tell Roo's story completely out of order—flashing back to her middle school years, forward to events of sophomore year, forward again to shrink appointments in which the events were discussed four months after they happened, etc.

Q. Readers often wonder how much an author is her main character. Are there any similarities between you and Ruby? Did you ever lose a friend over a boy?

A. All the events of the story are fictional. The element closest to true is Jackson's note-writing style. My first serious boyfriend used to write me notes like that and leave them in my mail cubby.

I used to live in Seattle, and the locations are largely real— the B&O Espresso, the U. District, etc. But Ruby's parents, her houseboat, her school, her various obsessions and interests— those are imaginary.

How am I like Roo? As a teenager, I was definitely a thrift-store maven. In both high school and college I was a scholarship kid surrounded by very wealthy people. I also have Roo's tendency to hyperanalyze small human interactions.

Yes, I have lost friends over boys—and boys to friends. I

wanted to write about heartbreak on more than one level—the heartbreak of losing a friend as well as the heartbreak of losing a boyfriend.

Q. "Tommy Hazard" has struck a chord with many readers. Did you have a Tommy Hazard? What was he like?

A. Tommy was actually an afterthought. I had a chapter that was too long and wanted to break it up, which meant I needed another boy—and I wanted to do something different than what I'd done in the other chapters.

I've been a little sad that so many girls love Tommy so much. Hello!?! Tommy Hazard and Prince Charming—neither one exists! You can't hold out for them or you will be sad and disappointed. Or you'll end up being the kind of girl (like Kim) who snatches other people's boyfriends because she's deluding herself that she's found perfection. Real boyfriends are real people. With flaws and often without glamour.

Q. The footnotes are a fun way to convey information. Where did you get the idea to use them? How did you decide what to put in them?

A. I've always liked footnotes. I trained to be an academic (I have a PhD in English literature) and I loved putting huge rambling asides in my footnotes while my central argument went on unimpeded by whatever tidbit had distracted my attention. I also love David Foster Wallace's essays, in which he uses copious and often hilarious footnotes. So I wanted to try using them to convey the inside of a teenage girl's mind.

How did I decide what to put in them? I wrote like a zillion and then my editor helped me figure out which ones were boring.

Q. Jackson is horrible at giving gifts. What is the best gift you've ever received from a boy? The worst?

A. The worst: Well, the half-carnation on Valentine's Day really did happen to me, my senior year of high school. But the worst gift ever was a USED OFFICE TELEPHONE (with several lines, etc.) that my boyfriend shoved, UNWRAPPED, under my pillow on Valentine's Day.

I already had a telephone.

This one involved wood veneer.

It was a random thing he found in the junk room of his office!

The best: There was a guy in college who later became my boyfriend. He graduated two or three years before me, and every now and then he used to just send me a letter, chatting about stuff. On my birthday one year, he sent me this tiny pin made out of a dead fish. It was a good-looking little fish, and it had been varnished or something, and mounted on a pin. I wouldn't wear it now, but at the time it seemed hilarious and punk rock and pretty all at the same time. It was small and it was a surprise, and I could tell he'd thought about my taste (questionable as it may have been). It worked much better than a dozen roses.

Q. Ruby loves movies, and the novel has fun movie references sprinkled throughout. What is your all-time top ten movie list?

A. I can't put them in order. Too stressful! But here's the list:
- *Gregory's Girl*
- *Repo Man*
- *Annie Hall*
- *Grease*
- *His Girl Friday*
- *Bringing Up Baby*

- *Cabaret*
- *Moulin Rouge*
- *Eternal Sunshine of the Spotless Mind*
- *Singin' in the Rain*

Q. This is your first novel for teenagers. Was there anything surprising about the process of writing it? Did you learn anything new?

A. I had a terrific amount of fun writing this book, but writing it was not so different from writing for adults or for younger kids, both of which I've done. I just try to write the best story I can.

Q. What were your favorite books as a teenager? Did any books or writers influence you while you were writing this book?

A. I read all the great early young adult authors when I was twelve and thirteen: Paul Zindel, S. E. Hinton, Judy Blume, M. E. Kerr. But I was more of a drama girl in high school and didn't read as much as I had in junior high. I fell back in love with books in college, reading great nineteenth-century novelists like Dickens, Austen, and the Brontës.

Writing *The Boyfriend List,* I was influenced by Nick Hornby's *High Fidelity,* which is about this guy who's always making lists and mix tapes. He goes back and visits his major old girlfriends to try to figure out what went wrong with his current relationship. I loved Hornby's book—it's tremendously clever and engaging—but parts of it didn't ring true for me. I thought there might be something fresh I could do with a similar concept.

Q. What is your writing process?

A. I write every weekday morning at my computer in my home office. A plump cat or two for company. More coffee than is good for me. I wear pajamas and look rather unattractive. I do not answer the phone, I do not clean the house, I check my e-mail only as a reward for doing my job. Sometimes I offer myself other ridiculous little rewards for writing—like: I can go out to the drugstore and buy toothpaste if I write two pages! It is borderline psychotic.

Q. What advice would you give to aspiring writers?

A. Go to college. Read as many books as you can. Try to get an internship at a publishing house or magazine. And write. It is very easy to say you are a writer and not write. But if you actually write stuff—then you are a writer, whether published or not.

The Boy Book • E. Lockhart • 978-0-385-73208-6

It's the beginning of Ruby Oliver's junior year at Tate Prep, and things are not off to a good start. But the year turns out to be full of surprises—along with many difficult decisions—that help Ruby see that there is indeed life outside the Tate universe.

Fly on the Wall • E. Lockhart • 978-0-385-73281-9

At the Manhattan School for Art and Music, where everyone is "different" and everyone is "special," Gretchen Yee feels ordinary. One day, Gretchen wishes she could be a fly on the wall in the boys' locker room—just to learn more about guys. (What are they really like? What do they really talk about?) This is the story of how that wish comes true.

Not Like I'm Jealous or Anything: The Jealousy Book
Edited by Marissa Walsh • 978-0-385-73317-5

We've all been there. We've all felt that pang. It's hard to stop the green-eyed monster once it rears its ugly head. In this collection of short stories, essays, and one poem, thirteen writers share their visions of jealousy.

Girl, 15, Charming but Insane • Sue Limb
978-0-385-73215-4

With her hilariously active imagination, Jess Jordan has a tendency to complicate her life, but now, as she's finally getting closer to her crush, she's determined to keep things under control. Readers will fall in love with Sue Limb's insanely optimistic heroine.

Counting Stars
David Almond
978-0-440-41826-9

With stories that shimmer and vibrate in the bright heat of memory, David Almond creates a glowing mosaic of his life growing up in a large, loving Catholic family in northeastern England.

The Sisterhood of the Traveling Pants
Ann Brashares
978-0-385-73058-7

Over a few bags of cheese puffs, four girls decide to form a sister-hood and take the vow of the Sisterhood of the Traveling Pants. The next morning, they say goodbye. And then the journey of the Pants, and the most memorable summer of their lives, begin.

The Second Summer of the Sisterhood
Ann Brashares
978-0-385-73105-8

With a bit of last summer's sand in the pockets, the Traveling Pants and the Sisterhood who wears them—Lena, Tibby, Bridget, and Carmen—embark on their second summer together.

Girls in Pants: The Third Summer of the Sisterhood
Ann Brashares
978-0-385-72935-2

It's the summer before the Sisterhood departs for college . . . their last real summer together before they head off to start their grown-up lives. It's the time when they need the Pants the most.

Walking Naked
Alyssa Brugman
978-0-440-23832-4

Megan Tuw has always been popular. But when she's thrown into detention with Perdita Wiguiggan, the most unpopular "freak" in school, Megan finds herself slowly drawn into an almost-friendship. Then Megan faces a choice: Perdita or the group?

Keeper of the Night
Kimberly Willis Holt
978-0-553-49441-9

Living on the island of Guam, a place lush with memories and tradition, young Isabel struggles to protect her family and cope with growing up after her mother's suicide.

The Lightkeeper's Daughter
Iain Lawrence
978-0-385-73127-0

Imagine growing up on a tiny island with no one but your family. For Squid McCrae, returning to the island after three years away unleashes a storm of bittersweet memories, revelations, and accusations surrounding her brother's death.

Lord of the Nutcracker Men
Iain Lawrence
978-0-440-41812-2

In 1914, Johnny's father leaves England to fight the Germans in France. With each carved wooden soldier he sends home, the brutality of war becomes more apparent. Soon Johnny fears that his war games foretell real battles and that he controls his father's fate.

Gathering Blue
Lois Lowry
978-0-440-22949-0

Lamed and suddenly orphaned, Kira is mysteriously taken to live in the palatial Council Edifice, where she is expected to use her gifts as a weaver to do the bidding of the all-powerful Guardians.

The Giver
Lois Lowry
978-0-440-23768-6

Jonas's world is perfect. Everything is under control. There is no war or fear or pain. There are no choices, until Jonas is given an opportunity that will change his world forever.

Harmony
Rita Murphy
978-0-440-22923-0

Power is coursing through Harmony—the power to affect the universe with her energy. This is a frightening gift for a girl who has always hated being different, and Harmony must decide whether to hide her abilities or embrace the consequences—good and bad—of her full strength.